From where did this woman get her class, her style, her apparently natural air of superiority? Her previous life couldn't have been one of tranquillity. She was forever on her guard.

"I wish you to go." Sonya gave an imperious flourish of her hand toward the door.

"Certainly." David rose to his splendid height, torn between anger and amusement. "You can show me out."

"I *will!*" There was an extraordinary intensity in her green eyes. Her body was alive with excitements, hungers. She moved swiftly ahead of him, so swiftly the tiny bow on one of her silver ballet shoes hooked on the fringe of the rug. She pitched forward and he caught her from behind.

His strong arms encircled her for the second time that day. Surrounded her like a force field. Her heart leaped into her throat as he pulled her back against him.

"David?" She tried to wrest away from him, but he held firm.

A certain contempt he felt for himself was no match for his desire for her. There had to be countless instances of overwhelming temptation, but he had never felt anything remotely like this before. There were only two possible options available to him. Let her go. Or give in to this furious passion.

Welcome to the
intensely emotional world of

Margaret Way

where rugged, brooding bachelors
meet their matches in the
burning heart of Australia....

Praise for the author

MARGARET WAY

In the Australian Billionaire's Arms

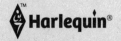

TORONTO NEW YORK LONDON
AMSTERDAM PARIS SYDNEY HAMBURG
STOCKHOLM ATHENS TOKYO MILAN MADRID
PRAGUE WARSAW BUDAPEST AUCKLAND

Recycling programs
for this product may
not exist in your area.

ISBN-13: 978-0-373-17722-6

IN THE AUSTRALIAN BILLIONAIRE'S ARMS

First North American Publication 2011

Copyright © 2011 by Margaret Way, Pty., Ltd.

This edition published by arrangement with Harlequin Books S.A.

For questions and comments about the quality of this book
please contact us at Customer_eCare@Harlequin.ca.

® and TM are trademarks of the publisher. Trademarks indicated with
® are registered in the United States Patent and Trademark Office, the
Canadian Trade Marks Office and in other countries.

www.eHarlequin.com

Printed in U.S.A.

Margaret Way, a definite Leo, was born and raised in the subtropical river city of Brisbane, capital of Queensland, the Sunshine State. A conservatorium-trained pianist, teacher, accompanist and vocal coach, she found that her musical career came to an unexpected end when she took up writing—initially as a fun thing to do. She currently lives in a harborside apartment at beautiful Raby Bay, a thirty-minute drive from the state capital, where she loves dining alfresco on her plant-filled balcony, overlooking a translucent-green marina filled with all manner of pleasure craft—from motor cruisers costing millions of dollars and big, graceful yachts with carved masts standing tall against the cloudless blue sky, to little bay runabouts. No one and nothing is in a mad rush, and she finds the laid-back village atmosphere very conducive to her writing. With well over one hundred books to her credit, she still believes her best is yet to come.

CHAPTER ONE

Such a beautiful young woman would always turn heads, Holt thought. Stares were guaranteed, and he was a man who automatically registered the physical details of anyone who crossed his path, whether business or social. He never forgot faces. He never forgot names. It was a God-given asset. Now his eyes were trained on the mystery woman as she entered the banquet room on the arm of Marcus Wainwright, the fifty-plus member of one of the richest and longest established families in the country. The combined impact brought the loud buzz of conversation in the huge room to an abrupt halt.

"I don't *believe* it!"

His date for the evening, Paula Rowlands, of Rowlands shopping malls fame, sounded as if she was on the verge of freaking out. "For crying out loud, Holt, that proves it! The gossip is *true*." For added emphasis, she dug her long nails into the fine cloth of his dinner jacket. "Marcus has brought her to the social event of the year."

That was enormously significant. "At least she didn't sneak in," he said dryly, "though I'm sure the toughest bouncer wouldn't have asked for ID. He'd have ushered her through with a 'wow!'"

Paula swung to face him. "Holt, really!" she chided. "She works in a *florist shop*!"

"There goes the neighbourhood!"

"God yes!" Paula moaned.

It was obvious Paula thought they were on the same page. It didn't occur to her he was being facetious. Paula was a snob. No doubt about it, but he liked her none the less. Snobbery was a minus, but Paula had a few pluses going for her. She was glamorous and generally good company both in and out of bed. The biggest plus for her among her wider circle of men friends was her billionaire father, George Rowlands. George was a genuine first-generation entrepreneur and a really decent guy. It was the Rowlands women, mother and daughter, Marilyn and Paula, neither of whom had worked a day in their lives apart from strenuous workouts in the gym, who suffered from delusions of grandeur.

"She *owns* the business, I believe," he tacked on. "Aunt Rowena told me only the other day when the rumours began to fly, she's a genius at handling flowers."

Paula stared at him with dumbstruck eyes. "Handling flowers, Holt? Darling, you can't be serious?"

He laughed. "Is that you in your Queen Victoria mode? Actually I am. I didn't say she pinched bucketloads from over neighbourhood fences and stacked them in the boot of her car. She apparently has a great talent for arranging flowers."

Paula continued to eye him incredulously. "How difficult is *that*?"

"Oh, believe me, it's an art form. It really is." Hadn't he pondered over what precisely had gone wrong with Marilyn Rowlands's many unsuccessful attempts at the Rowlands mansion?

"Joe the goose can arrange flowers," Paula said complacently, supremely unaware she had inherited her mother's "eye". "The trick is to buy lots, then shove them in fancy vases."

"Too easy!" He continued to track the progress of Marcus and the beauty on his arm. She might have walked out of a bravura late nineteenth century painting, he decided, his attention well and truly caught. Singer Sargent or Jacque Emile Blanche perhaps? A lover of beauty in all its forms, for a moment he damned nearly forgot where he was. Small wonder Marcus had become infatuated.

"Your great-aunt here tonight?" Paula asked, hoping the answer was no. Rowena Wainwright-Palmerston rather intimidated Paula, though she knew it wasn't deliberate. "She looks great for her age," she said in an unconsciously patronising voice.

"Rowena looks great for *any* age," Holt clipped off smartly, though his attention was fully employed studying the blonde vision.

"Holt, baby?" Paula elbowed him in the ribs, trying to draw his attention back to her.

He had to grimace. "What are you trying to do, maim me?"

"Never!" She began to rhythmically smooth his back with her hands.

"She's extremely beautiful." He felt a stab of alarm. He was very fond of Marcus. Protective as well. Whatever he had expected of Marcus's shock lady friend, it wasn't this, though his great-aunt had warned him.

"She's quite a remarkable young lady and, without question, well bred. Cool old-style beauty, if you know what I mean. Very Mittel Europa. Not a modern look at all. That would appeal to Marcus. There's a story there, mark my words!"

"I hope you noticed the *hair*?" A bridling Paula jolted him out of his thoughts again.

"You're not going to tell me *you* were born with copper hair?"

Paula's eyes flashed with resentment. "Just a few foils," she lied. "Hers can't be real! Where do you get that *white* blonde except from a bottle?"

"Scandinavia, maybe?" he suggested. "Her surname is Erickson, I believe. Sonya Erickson. Bit of a clue. Norwegian background perhaps? Norway the Land of the Midnight Sun, birthplace of Ibsen, Grieg, Edvard Munch, Sigrid Undset, and, as I recall, the infamous Quisling."

Paula frowned. She didn't know half those people. She'd seen Ibsen's *Hedda Gabler* at the Sydney Theatre Company and thought it a dead bore, even if Cate Blanchett was as always brilliant. So far as she was concerned the play had little or no relevance to modern life. And what sort of a solution was suicide? "I never thought Marcus could be such a fool," she said with surprising bitterness. "Neither did Mummy."

"Ah, Mummy!" The *terrible* Mummy who had a Chihuahua called Mitzi that greeted male visitors in full Rottweiler mode. Marilyn Rowlands, who had been brought up to believe if a girl wasn't married by twenty-four she was doomed to live and die alone. Marilyn was therefore desperate to marry off her twenty-eight-year-old daughter.

To *him*.

Even if Paula were the last woman left in the world, he feared he would remain a bachelor.

"You were at the dinner party Mummy arranged to get Marcus and Susan Hampstead together, remember?" Paula took condemnatory eyes off Ms Ericksen to shoot him a glance. "They'd both lost their partners."

His reply was terse to the point of curtness. "Susan Hampstead. *Three* marriages? *Three* divorces? Marcus lost his dearly loved wife." There was a world of difference between the late Lucy Wainwright and Susan Hampstead, a living, breathing, career courtesan, and he wasn't going to let Paula forget it.

"Yes, yes, I *know*." Paula resumed rubbing his back in a conciliatory and, it had to be said, irritatingly *proprietary* fashion. He couldn't embarrass her in public by shrugging her off. He had to stand there and take it. They weren't an Item. He had been up front about it all. *No* commitment, but try as he did he couldn't stop Paula and her mother thinking there was or there would very soon be.

His mood turned pensive. "Marcus has been a very sad man for a long time. It's good to see him out and about." Only the *last* thing the Wainwright clan would want for Marcus was to make a dreadful and inevitably painful mistake. The girl was too young. Too beautiful. Too everything. She mightn't have Susan Hampstead's cobra-like attack, but in real terms she could prove far more dangerous.

"Marcus obviously footed the bill for her dress." Paula glanced down at her own stunning designer gown, which suddenly appeared to her less stunning. "I can imagine just how much that evening dress cost. No florist could possibly afford it. It's couture. Vintage Chanel, I'd say. The jewellery too. Surely I've seen the pendant before?"

Mummy certainly would have, he thought, but he didn't enlighten Paula. The pendant necklace, an exquisite Colombian emerald surrounded by a sunburst of diamonds, that hung around the girl's white swan neck had belonged to Lucy. So too had the chandelier-style diamond earrings. The set had been Marcus's wedding gift to his beautiful green-eyed wife. They hadn't been seen for the best part of six years, which was roughly the time lovely little Lucy had taken to die of bone cancer.

"Ah, well, mistresses never go out of date." His own

surge of resentment towards the newcomer shocked him. *Lucy's emeralds, God!* Would Lucy mind? Would she turn over in her grave? No, Lucy had been a beautiful person. Shouldn't he at least give this young woman a chance? But his male intuition had gone into overdrive. She was one of those life altering women. Needless to say she would be very clever. Manipulative, as a matter of course. He noted she had matched her gown, not only to the jewel, but to her beautiful emerald eyes. They were set at a fascinating slant. Her eyes rivalled the precious gemstone. It dipped into the perfectly arched upper swells of her breasts. Her skin was flawless, lily white. One rarely saw such porcelain skin outside Europe. Her beautiful, thick, white-blonde hair, which he was prepared to bet a million dollars was natural with that white skin, was arranged in an elegant chignon interwoven with silver and gold threads that stood out like a glittering sunburst. It was incredibly effective. They could have had a young goddess on the scene.

Rowena as usual was spot on. A young woman who owned and worked in a florist shop looked like Old World aristocracy, so regal was her demeanour. She didn't appear in the least overawed by her lavish surroundings, the fashionable crowd, the seriously rich, the celebrities and socialites, or troubled by the full-on battery of stares. She moved with confidence showing no sign she was aware of the effect she was having on the room full of guests. Royalty couldn't have pulled it off better.

"And she's got inches on Marcus," Paula pointed out, as though it were absolutely *verboten* for a woman to be taller than her escort.

"Very likely her high heels." She was certainly above average height for a woman. As a couple, they were a study in contrasts. Marcus, medium height, worryingly thin, dark, grey-flecked hair, grey eyes, an austere scholarly face, and a knife sharp brain. He looked more like a university don than a captain of industry. His companion was ultra slender, but not in that borderline anorexic way Holt so disliked. She was *willowy*. She moved beautifully with the grace of a trained dancer. Lovely arms, neck and small high breasts. Her legs, hidden by the full-length silk gown, would no doubt be just as spectacular.

That as may be, she couldn't be the defunct European aristocrat she appeared. More likely a hard-nosed gold-digger lurking beneath the surface. A woman as beautiful as that could have any man she wanted. Obviously topping her list of requirements for potential suitors was considerable *wealth*. That would decimate the numbers. Though Marcus was by no means the richest member of the Wainwright family—that was the family patriarch, Julius—Marcus had at least a hundred and forty million dollars. A fortune that size assured any man up to ninety years of age blue-chip eligibility. A hundred and forty million dollars should just about cover any girl-on-the-make's lifetime expenses.

Paula got another steely grip on his arm.

"Hey, Paula, those sessions at the gym are really paying off."

"Sorry." She relaxed the pressure. "You're not usually so testy. But I guess you're upset for poor Marcus. She's obviously an adventuress."

"A lot of women have that streak."

Paula gave a nervous laugh. At least she was an heiress. That let her off the hook. "Look out," she warned, clearly perturbed. "They're coming *our* way,"

He gave her a sardonic glance. "Why not? Marcus is my uncle, after all."

She recognised him from his photographs. David Holt Wainwright. They didn't do him justice. In the flesh he was the embodiment of vibrant masculinity. Oddly enough a lot of handsome men were lacking in that department. He had it in spades. A kind of devilish dazzle, she thought. Handsome was too tame a word. She took in the height, the splendid physique, that look of high intelligence he shared with his uncle, the infinite self confidence only the super-rich had, plus an intrinsic sexiness that from all accounts drew women in droves. His thick crow-black hair, worn a little longer than usual, was cut into deep crisp waves that clung to his well-shaped skull. His brilliant dark eyes, so dark a brown they appeared black, dominated his dynamic face. He photographed well. A flashing white smile that lit a dark face to radiance was a big asset for anyone in the public eye. But the glossy images were as nothing to the man.

And he had already arrived at the conclusion she was an adventuress looking for a rich husband. It was there in that brilliant assessing gaze. What greater legitimacy could there be for a working girl than to marry a millionaire?

"David's friend is Paula Rowlands," Marcus was murmuring quietly in her ear. "Her father owns a good many shopping malls. Don't let her rattle you."

"Does it matter what she thinks of me?" she asked calmly, grateful she had mastered the art of hiding her true feelings to a considerable degree. It had been a struggle concealing her vulnerabilities, but she had learned to her cost to be very wary of trusting people, let alone sharing her innermost thoughts. Marcus, a lovely man, was the outstanding exception.

"No, it doesn't." Marcus laughed.

"Well, then." She hugged his arm. Being here tonight had everything to do with her respect and affection for Marcus Wainwright. She knew in accepting his invitation she was making a big shift out of obscurity into the limelight. It didn't sit comfortably with her but Marcus had insisted her appearance would be remarked on and bring in a whole lot of new customers. For some time now she had started to number the rich among her regulars. Most had lovely manners, others were unbelievably pretentious. Marcus's aunt Rowena, Lady Palmerston, widow of the distinguished British diplomat of the late seventies early eighties, Sir Roland Palmerston, was among the former. She frequently called into the shop, saying delightedly she found Sonya's arrangements "inspiring".

"But she'll try, my dear," Marcus warned. "The Rowlands women are frightful snobs. *Money* is their aristocracy."

"Your nephew must see something in her? She's very attractive and she has a real flair for wearing clothes."

Marcus gave a dry laugh that turned into a cough. "My nephew wants and needs a great deal more than that in a woman. It's Paula and her mother who hang in there."

"Well, he *is* seriously eligible," she put forward with a smile.

"David got the best of all of us," he said with very real pride.

The cautionary voice always at work inside Sonya's head was issuing warnings. Not of the smug-faced Paula Rowlands, heiress, but David Holt Wainwright, Marcus's dearly loved nephew. *He* was the one who was going to cause her grief. She had learned to rely on her intuition. David Wainwright was a very important figure in Marcus's life. He was already querying the exact nature of her friendship with Marcus. And friendship was all it was. She had her suspicions Marcus wanted more of her. He could offer her a great deal, not the least of it blessed *safety*, but at this point she was allowing the friendship plenty of time to go where it would.

* * *

Afterwards it seemed to Holt that Sonya Erickson had entered his life in a kind of blaze. Very few people did that. It wasn't just her beauty, ravishing though it was, it was the inbred self-confidence. Beauty alone didn't guarantee that kind of self-assurance. Paula didn't have it for all her privileged background. This young woman was the very picture of patrician ease. There had to be a whole file on her somewhere with many secrets lodged therein. Paula was still whispering in his ear, for all she was worth, even though Marcus and his beautiful companion were almost upon them.

"Do me a favour, Paula, okay?" He put a staying hand on her arm.

"Of course, darling. Whatever you say!"

"Then kindly shut up. It's damned rude."

Holt made the move forward, his hand extended, a natural smile of great charm on his face. "Uncle Marcus."

"David." A matching expression of deepest affection lit the older man's face.

The two shook hands, then moved into their usual hug. Marcus and Lucille Wainwright had not been blessed with children, though they had longed for them. Holt had been very close to both from childhood as a result. They loved him. He loved them. In a way he had been the son they never had.

Marcus began the introductions the moment they broke apart. "Sonya Erickson." No further explanation. Just Sonya Erickson. No more was offered. But it was painfully obvious Sonya Erickson had become extremely important to him. If not, why the emeralds?

Remember Lucy's emeralds.

"*Sonya*, please," the young woman invited as she gave Holt her hand. It was done so gracefully—hang on, so *regally*—he was a beat away from raising her elegant hand just short of his lips. That caused a moment of black amusement. Yet there wasn't the merest hint of seduction in her beautiful green eyes when so many women tried it on. There wouldn't be a woman in the country who didn't know he had a few bob. But Ms Erickson's glorious green eyes revealed nothing beyond an aristocratic interest and a cool speculation to match his.

Up close she was even more beautiful. Paula, brightly chatting now to Marcus—Step Two in Paula's plan was to charm all his relatives—must be *hating* her. Beautiful women were a major stumbling block to their less fortunate sisters. Another man might have been overwhelmed. Not he. He had his head well and truly screwed on. But admittedly he was a man who recognised the fact a woman's beauty was immensely powerful. The beautiful Sonya had gained Marcus's attention. No mean feat. Marcus wasn't the kind of man who'd had passing affairs after Lucy's death. Rather Marcus had turned into something of a recluse.

Now this! Ms Erickson had mesmerized him. If Holt stood looking into her green eyes much longer, it might well happen to him, such was her spectacular allure.

"Marcus speaks of you often," she was saying, snapping him back to attention.

"If I need someone to speak well of me I go to Marcus," he said.

"I wondered if perhaps I should have curtsied?" Sonya smiled at him with aloof charm.

"Maybe I would have returned a bow. Here's to beauty!"

"No wonder Marcus loves you," she murmured.

He couldn't resist. "And he obviously finds you special."

That self-confidence, the patrician air, just *had* to be inbred. He began to wonder about her background. Might be an idea to check it out. Who *was* she? She had a lovely speaking voice to add to her assets. A faint accent. He couldn't pick it up. Surely indicated a gracious background? Or an intensive course in elocution. Did they still call it that? *Elocution, art of speech?*

His hand, he found to his mild self-disgust, was still feeling the effect of its contact with her skin. It was like a brief but searing encounter with electricity. It sent sparkles racing up his arm and a stir through his body. He had to take note. The lady was dangerous. She rated attention.

"Marcus is very dear to me," he said, taking just enough care that it didn't sound like a warning.

"Then you are both blessed."

She turned away from him to Marcus, a hint of sadness in her face.

A woman of mystery indeed!

And didn't she know how to play the part! In fact she was so good it was all he could do not to applaud.

Paula, momentarily sidelined, pushed herself back into the conversation with a smile. "May I say how beautiful you look, Ms Erickson." She couldn't quite pull genuine sincerity off.

"Thank you." A slight inclination of the white-blonde head.

Paula had to be an idiot if she didn't realize the mysterious Ms Erickson had summed her up on the spot and decided to shrug off the underlying hostility and dislike. Wise move, he thought. Play it cool.

"And the necklace!" Paula, big on jewellery, threw up both hands. "It's absolutely *glorious*! You must tell me how you came by it. A family heirloom perhaps?"

Zero tact on Paula's part. She might as well have shouted: *As though that's possible!*

Just as he was debating abandoning Paula for the

evening or perhaps treading on her expensively shod toe, Ms Erickson put her long-fingered white hand very lightly to the great glittering emerald. "My family lost everything at the end of World War Two," she offered very gravely.

God, that woman, Anna Andersen, claiming to be the Grand Duchess Anastasia couldn't have done it any better, Holt thought. Why on earth would she want to be a florist? She had everything going for her to be a big movie star.

"Really?" Paula exclaimed, incredulously.

He could read Paula's thoughts. Ms Erickson was only making it up.

"That *can't* be true! I feel you're kidding me."

"Too true." Sonya Erickson's reply was so quiet she might have been talking to herself.

High time to step in. The last thing he ever wanted was to offer the slightest embarrassment to his uncle.

"Shall we go to our table?" he suggested. His voice was as smooth as molasses, when his blood was heating up.

Marcus, who had tensed, gently took hold of the exquisite Sonya's arm. "Lead the way, David," he murmured.

He did so, shouldering responsibility like a man.

Since Marcus had pressed her to accompany him to this gala evening Sonya had wondered what it would be like. Now her gaze swept across the spacious room. Everything sparkled under the big chandeliers: glittering sequins, beading, crystals, expensive jewellery, smiling eyes. And the dresses! Strapless, one-shouldered, backless, daringly near frontless. A kaleidoscope of colour. She had known she would be mixing with the super rich, people in the public eye, and perhaps she would be meeting a member or two of Marcus's family, although she knew his parents were currently in New York. She knew all about David Holt Wainwright. She had gleaned quite a lot from magazines and business reviews. He was very highly regarded, brilliant in fact, the man to watch even though she knew he wasn't yet thirty. His mother was Sharron Holt-Wainwright, heiress to Holt Pharmaceuticals. Money married money. That was the way of it. Marcus always referred to his nephew as David. Mostly he got *Holt* from his mother's family and just about everyone else, Marcus had explained. It was his uncle Philip, his mother's brother, who had hit on the nickname. It had stuck, probably because the arresting good looks and the superior height had come from the Holt side of the family.

She felt Marcus's family would be against her. The age difference would be a big factor although rich men married beautiful young women all the time. Whether such marriages were for love or not, young wives were rarely given the benefit of the doubt. That was the way of the world. The gossip would have gone out. She worked in a florist shop, a good one, but she wasn't someone from their social milieu. She was a working girl. No one of any account. No esteemed family. No connections. No background of prestigious schools and university. Worse yet, she was twenty-five. Marcus was almost three decades on, not to mention his wealth. By and large, she had accepted the invitation against her better judgment. She knew her blonde beauty, inherited from her mother and maternal grandmother, gave her a real shot at power, but she had never entertained the notion she could land herself a millionaire.

Marcus was different. She had sensed the unresolved grief in him from the very first time he had wandered into her shop. He had been lingering outside, a distinguished older man, impeccably dressed, looking in the window, enticed apparently by an arrangement of lime-green lilium buds and luxurious tropical leaves, figs on branches, and some wonderful ruby-red peonies she had arranged in an old Japanese wooden vase. Just the one arrangement. No distractions.

She had smiled at him, catching his eyes. A moment later he came into the shop filled with beautiful flowers and exquisite scents. A shyly elegant, courtly man. She had taken to him on the spot. Trace memories, she supposed. The *friendship* had flourished. These days he allowed her to "work her magic" in his very beautiful home. It was way too big for a man on his own—a mansion. He employed a married couple, housekeeper and chauffeur/groundsman, who lived in staff quarters in the grounds but he had long refused to sell the house when many spectacular offers had been made. The house he had shared with his late wife. It held all his memories.

She knew all about memories. It had cemented their bond. It was just one of those things that happened in life. Like called to like. Marcus had later directed his aunt, Lady Palmerston, to her shop. Lady Palmerston in turn had directed many of her friends. She owed them both a lot. She realized for any young woman, especially one in her position, Marcus Wainwright would be a great catch. His age wouldn't come into it. He was a handsome, highly intelligent and very interesting man. He was also the type of man who liked making the people in his life happy. Self-gratification wasn't his thing. Marcus was a fine man. The first time she had met him he had commented on her green eyes.

"My late wife had wonderful eyes too. Green as emeralds."

Poor Marcus with all his dreams of happiness shot down in flames. Similar tragedies had happened to her.

"What are you thinking about?"

Sonya turned her head towards that vibrant, very sexy voice. It was pitched low for her ears only. All through the lavish four-course dinner she had listened with fascinated attention to his contributions to the conversation. It volleyed back and forth between highly educated, professional people. Even so, it was Holt Wainwright who carried their table of eight along effortlessly. He had a wide range of interests about which he was very knowledgeable. He was highly articulate and quick witted. He effortlessly commanded an impressive company. And here was a man, easily the youngest man at the table, totally at ease and in control of himself. She had to give him full marks for that.

She had been seated between Marcus and Holt. Marcus was busy answering a flurry of questions from one of the women guests, Tara Bradford, a top executive with a merchant bank, a formidable looking woman in her well-preserved early fifties. Sonya caught the vibes. Not that it was difficult. Tara Bradford, a divorcee, tall, thin, handsome more than attractive, was very interested in Marcus. She showed it in every look, every gesture. Tara had been a close friend of Marcus's late wife. She had directed only a few words Sonya's way, but with a smooth courtesy. Public relations were important. Tara gave the strong impression she already knew Marcus would come to his senses. May-November matches were just so unsuitable. Besides, the mature woman had so much more to offer.

Sonya, for her part, had been intensely aware of Holt Wainwright. Nothing extraordinary about that. He was a very charismatic man. Scores of women would have felt his attraction. She wasn't about to become enmeshed in such madness. But one couldn't control chemical reactions. Mercifully caution had been inbred in her. Getting too close to Holt Wainwright would be like playing with fire. Any resultant conflagration could pull the life she had so carefully constructed for herself down on her head. That kind of insight lent an edge of fear, like a glittering sword poised over her head.

Holt sat in silence watching the gentle tenderness of her expression gradually change. It lost its warmth, became almost shuttered. "I was recalling how I first met Marcus," she told him lightly.

"He came into your florist shop." His smile was urbane, but his instincts were every bit as keen as hers. He knew at some level they could hurt one another badly. Hurt Marcus. A little danger always excited him, but that couldn't happen with Marcus involved. He cared far too much about his uncle.

Sonya wasn't about to allow his brilliant fathoms-deep dark gaze faze her. "But you *know*. Marcus was attracted to one of my arrangements in the window."

"I'm told you're a genius at work."

"A quiet achiever!" she said, finding it difficult to unlock her glance from his. They had become almost duel-like in quality. "Lady Palmerston?"

"Another one of your admirers."

"Thankfully." Her expression relaxed into a smile. "I run a business. I need customers. Good customers who appreciate what I do."

"Then you must have been thrilled Marcus and my great-aunt walked through your door," he returned suavely.

She looked directly into his clever, probing eyes. "Perhaps I can help *you* at some time, David. I've begun arranging the flowers for luncheons, dinner parties, parties of all kinds, weddings. I've had to take on staff."

As if he'd be rash enough to make a booking! "I'll make note of that," he said, knowing full well he would never contact her. Too dangerous. Better to lie awake thinking about it. "Tell me about yourself," he invited.

And wouldn't there be lots to tell, said the cynical voice in his head.

"Little to tell." She had no difficulty with the lie. "Anyway, I'm sure you'll run a few checks."

"I'm your man," he said with cool amusement.

"There is such a thing as minding your own business." She drew back a little, picking up her wine glass.

"The thing is, Sonya, beautiful exotic women usually have a few skeletons in the cupboard."

"A cynical view."

"Truer than you think."

"Then it's a great comfort to me to know, if I do have a few skeletons lurking in my cupboard, *you* won't find them." There was a blend of mockery and disdain in her voice.

"Is that a dare?"

"What can I say?" She shrugged her white shoulders.

Beautiful shoulders. He could learn to appreciate that shrug. Even wait for it. And that little gesture with her hands? Pure *Europa.* "Yes, or no," he said.

She dared turn her head knowing he was baiting her. His eyes were as dark as hers were full of light. "No dare. It's a promise," she replied, keeping her voice as low pitched as his.

At the same moment Marcus turned his attention back to Sonya with what looked like an expression of relief on his face. Surely Tara knew she would never land Marcus? Holt thought. Lucy and Tara had been friends. It was clear poor Tara thought that guaranteed her next in line. Though even Tara would be far more suitable than Ms Erickson of the emerald-green eyes. If he had panicked her in any way she hid it supremely well. How did she manage such aplomb at twenty-five years of age?

He knew in his bones he was right. Ms Sonya Erickson had a *past*.

Right now she was looking to a rosy future with Marcus. He hadn't a single doubt if she wanted marriage she would get it. She was already wearing the jewels. He needed to ask Marcus in a diplomatic way if he had lent them to her for the night. Or had he gone totally overboard and given them to her? That idea plagued him. He imagined the sort of conversation that might have gone on.

"You're wearing an emerald silk dress, Sonya? I have in mind a particular necklace and matching earrings. They need an airing, after being locked away in the safe."

Did she protest? *"Really, no, Marcus!"*

"It would please me so much."

To be strictly fair it was hard to resist Marcus. Maybe she was the sort of young woman who lived to please. Dear Marcus, so long faithful to the memory of his beautiful Lucy, appeared to have fallen deeply in love.

Alas!

No wonder writers used the verb *fall*. The feeling was exactly like a free fall through space. The profound worry was the beautiful Sonya could be the best heartbreaker of them all. She must have trodden a path littered with admirers. *Lovers?* Despite himself he thought it would be quite an experience to share a bed with Ms Erickson. He was only human, but he was having none of taking Ms Erickson on trust. The beautiful Ms Erickson was wearing a mask. He would check on her discreetly. Clarify the situation.

The voice in his head said wryly, *It's already too late.*

CHAPTER TWO

MIDWEEK Holt had lunch with Rowena. Usual place, Simone's. The food was so good even Gordon Ramsay would have to wax lyrical. He and Rowena had things to discuss. Namely Marcus's future. Marcus was very dear to both of them and now they realized Marcus for the second time in his life was totally enraptured and could be at that very moment seriously considering marrying a woman young enough to be his daughter.

Okay, was that a bad thing? It happened all the time with beautiful clever girls. Most often they were blonde. Rich men married blondes for choice. He didn't exactly know why. Beauty came in many guises. But he had to say blonde was good.

He was nearly ten minutes late, having to work hard at winding up a meeting with a lot of guys in business suits and one woman executive with really Big Hair. With the light behind her he had the unsettling sensation he was talking to a balloon. If he lived to be one hundred he would still be amazed by what women did to their hair. The incredible colours they tried out. One of the girls in the office, Ellie, had gone briefly pink and purple. Maybe it was to attract his attention? He had stumbled over her so often, he had come to the conclusion she deliberately lay in wait.

A majestic-looking Rowena waved when she saw him, her face lighting up.

"Sorry I'm late." He threaded his way through the tables, acknowledging friends along the way. Simone's did a roaring trade with the big end of town. He bent to kiss Rowena's velvet cheek. He loved everything about her. Her wit and her wisdom. She always wore the same perfume like a signature note. Roses softened by iris, musk and, he thought, vanilla? It was so wonderfully subtle and evocative of Rowena, who could blame her for sticking to one sublime perfume? Most of the women in his circle ran the gamut. The beautiful Sonya had worn a serenely beautiful fragrance he was not familiar with. But it had been heaven to inhale.

"What are we having?" Once seated, he picked up the menu.

Rowena glanced across at him, delighting in his handsomeness. "I hope I did the right thing, dear. I've already ordered for both of us. I know how little time you have."

"You also know my tastes. So what is it?" He put up his hand to signal the drinks waiter. He and Rowena always shared a bottle of wine. Just enough. Not too much. He had plenty of work to do. Rowena, after a long successful life as a top diplomat's wife and hostess, knew exactly her limits. He only wished Paula did. She had become very argumentative after the gala night, claiming Sonya Erickson had not only sunk her claws in Marcus but had fascinated *him* as well. Of course he had denied it. Not strenuously.

To go with the fine Riesling Rowena had chosen seared scallops, white truffle butter, Tasmanian salmon with a creamy crab sauce and niçoise vegetables; he said he'd pass on dessert. Rowena elected to stay with the chocolate and mandarin parfait. Rowena was one of those fortunate women who loved her food but never put on a pound.

"So, you think Marcus is in love with her?" Rowena got right down to business.

"I wouldn't say it if I didn't. She's extremely beautiful. Well spoken. And nobody's fool."

"But you don't trust her?" Rowena had the Wainwright piercing grey eyes.

"What do *you* think?"

"I haven't seen them together, dear."

"Excuse me, do you have to? She was wearing *Lucy's emeralds*! Not something I'd expect of Marcus."

"Maybe she promised to take them off when the night was over." Rowena gave him an arch smile.

"Do you suppose she *stayed* over?" The idea dismayed him. Not a good sign.

"Come on, my dear. You sound dismal. It's the twenty-first century. Marcus is still a fine-looking man. She could well have."

"Then he's a lucky son of a gun," he said, with a twist in his smile.

"Sure you weren't a bit taken yourself?" She reached out to touch his hand.

"I'm a *man*, Rowena," he said very dryly.

"Very much so. What about that Paula of yours?"

He ran a hand over his brow. "Rowena, you *know* perfectly well Paula is a long-time friend. It's not serious."

"God, I hope not!" Rowena heaved a grateful sigh. "And that mother of hers!" She closed her eyes. "I bet she never gets off her knees praying for a match. But enough of the Rowlands. No wonder poor George spends his entire time at work."

"I like him."

"So do I." Rowena smiled. "A diamond in the rough."

"Ms Erickson is no rough diamond," he pointed out. "She has the aristocrat down pat. She's highly intelligent.

And ultra cool. But she doesn't love Marcus. That's the big worry."

"How would *you* know?" Rowena's gaze sharpened on his face.

"I *know*," he said and glanced away.

"So you're worried where this is going?"

"The short answer, Rowena, darling, is *yes*. I'd be a fool not to be wary of Ms Erickson."

"For what it's worth, I like her. I *really* like her."

"Your opinion is worth a lot. But what's her story?" he asked tersely. "She has one, of course."

Rowena nodded sagely. "One wouldn't have to be a mastermind to sense that. She has a very graceful flow of conversation. Pick a subject. Any subject. She speaks fluent French. I once put a question to her in French about the extraordinary arrangement she was working on at the time, a blend of burgundy and pale pink calla lilies. She answered, switching automatically from English to French. Polished accent. Better than mine. The one thing she doesn't talk about is herself. She appears so self-contained yet I feel she's terribly *alone*. There's a sadness there, don't you think?"

"Maybe that's part of her role of woman of mystery?" His tone was highly sceptical. "She could be a consummate actress."

Rowena negated that with a shake of her silver-streaked head. "She's genuine."

"But genuine what, Rowena dear? I've made a few enquiries on the side. Couldn't come up with anything much. I might try Interpol." It was only half a joke.

"She's only been in the country for around five years," Rowena supplied.

"Yes, I found out that much. There's a trace of an accent that isn't French."

"Hungarian," Rowena said with some certainty.

"Hungarian?" He set down his wine glass to give her a long look. Rowena and her husband had lived for many years in Europe. "The land of Liszt, Bela Bartok, Kodaly, Franz Lehar? I've even heard of the gorgeous Gabor sisters and their equally gorgeous mother. You know I haven't visited Budapest, which you assure me is one of the most beautiful cities in Europe, but you and Sir Roland knew it well. Or did you ask her straight out?"

"No, love." Rowena sat back. "But I have an excellent ear for accents. Besides, Sonya is a very private young lady. Her inbuilt cautions, insecurities if you like, have something to do with her former life. Somehow she has developed—"

"A mask?" he supplied. "So what is the mask hiding?"

Rowena sighed. "I'm having one of my buffet luncheons next Sunday. I'm asking Sonya. Would you care to come?"

He decided on the spot to *seize* on the invitation. Worry about the collateral damage later. "Is Marcus coming?"

"I wanted to speak to you first, before giving him a call. I always ask Marcus. He comes if he likes the people."

"Oh, God, Rowena," he groaned. "I advise extreme caution. I have the feeling the beautiful Sonya is going to wheel out a trolley full of tricks."

"Possibly," Rowena considered. "But I like her and I do love a mystery. So do you."

"If only she were older!" he lamented. "More suitable."

"No, no, *no* to Tara Bradford." Rowena threw up her hands in horror.

"Tara wouldn't break his heart," he pointed out rather grimly.

"What a blessing." Rowena allowed herself a touch of malice. "Only Marcus has no romantic interest in poor old

Tara. Wishful thinking on her part. She's a splendid woman in many ways, but she does have thunderous legs."

"All the better to hold her up," he offered vaguely. "I haven't seen Sonya's legs yet. I bet they're perfect."

Rowena nodded. "I have and they *are*."

The following afternoon he stopped by Marcus's house with its millions-plus view of Sydney Harbour. He'd been extremely busy all week with meetings plus endless piles of paperwork his father usually handled. His father, a notoriously secretive man, and CEO of Wainwright Enterprises, trusted few people outside his immediate family. These days he was leaving more and more to his only son and heir, adding to his already heavy workload. As a consequence he hadn't had a chance to catch up with his uncle, who headed up the property department. Considering the properties owned by Wainwright Enterprises, it was a huge job in itself. As well, he and Marcus, both of them holding Law and Economics degrees with first-class honours, sat in on major meetings with the legal department. They did work in the same building, Wainwright Towers, but not on the same floor. Made a surprising difference as it happened.

The house Marcus and Lucy had lived in for so many years had been left to Lucy by her maternal grandmother, Lady Marina Harnett, a great philanthropist and art collector. To Holt's eye it was one of the prettiest houses in the city. Not grand like the Wainwright ancestral home he had been raised in, but smaller and more welcoming to his eye, especially in the days when Aunt Lucy had been alive. She was the sweetest, kindest woman imaginable and she had to die. That was the trouble with life; there was always death at the end. The enemy that couldn't be overcome. Death did despicable things. He remembered his mother had been grief stricken when at long last Lucy had passed away. She and Lucy had been great friends. The family had taken Lucy to their hearts. No one could take her place.

So what *now*, with a very possible candidate for the second Mrs Marcus Wainwright on the scene? Would it be seen by the family as a betrayal of Lucy? Everyone wanted Marcus's happiness, but a beautiful young woman like Sonya Erickson could only inspire suspicion. God help him, he was already dealing with his mistrust of her.

He stepped out of the car, glancing briefly at a small blue hatchback nosed into a corner. Looked as if the estate had bought the housekeeper a new little runabout. The gardens were looking superb, ablaze with flowers. He started across the paved circular drive to the sandstone house. It had been built in the mid-1850s to a very high standard. Regency in design, it was perfectly symmetrical. The only concession to the Australian climate was the broad verandah with its series of white elegant pillars and fretwork. A lot of the original land had been sold off over the years—too valuable for one family to keep to themselves—but the original servants' quarters, beautifully maintained and updated, were still at the rear of the house along with storerooms that looked more like bungalows. He had spent such a lot of time here, for a moment he was overwhelmed by nostalgia.

"David, darling."

Pulled tight by little Aunt Lucy—a bare inch or so over five feet—feeling the great affection she had for him break over him in waves. No wonder Marcus had turned into himself after he lost her. Life could be very cruel. Sometimes it appeared as though the best went early. It would take for ever for the Wainwright clan to accept someone like Sonya if the worst came to the worst. A beautiful young woman's motives for marrying a man old enough to be her father could *not* be pure. He had felt her affection for

Marcus. That was genuine enough. The huge worry was it would take a miracle for that affection to turn to love. At least romantic love. Didn't every young woman want that? Didn't every young man? He was moving fast towards thirty. Many attractive young women had come his way but no one who engaged him in every possible way. He really wanted that. He wanted passion. He wanted magic. He wanted a woman to capture his imagination. Sadly no one ever had. He was beginning to wonder if anyone ever would.

That was what he wanted. He wanted the right woman to bring fulfilment to his existence. Not that he didn't have a good life. A very busy life, a privileged life, but he knew what he was missing. His mother and father had been greatly blessed with a love match. He had grown up in a happy, stable household fully aware of how much his parents loved one another and him. It greatly disturbed him now to realize he was only a nudge away from maybe wanting to be where Sonya Erickson was. No use telling himself it was because he needed to check her out for Marcus's sake. So where did that leave him?

In an impossible position, pal.

There lay the answer. His love for his uncle was deep. He could never be the one to hurt him. As for Sonya? Wouldn't it be natural for any young woman to be flattered by the attentions of an older, rich and distinguished man? Even have her head temporarily turned? The worrying thing was Ms Erickson revealed no such excitements. She was entirely in possession of herself when excitement, even joy, fitted much better. He was well advised to mistrust her. His allegiance was to Marcus.

The front door was open. He was about to call a hello when a young woman came into sight carrying a large crystal bowl filled with a profusion of beautiful flowers.

He didn't register the full array of blossoms, gerberas, lush roses, peonies, he was too busy concentrating on the young woman. She wore fitted jeans that showed off her lovely lissom figure and the length of her legs. A simple vest-type top did the same for her breasts. Her shimmering long hair, centre parted, fell down her back in thick sinuous coils.

Rapunzel.

She came to a halt, so clearly startled he might have been wearing a balaclava over his head.

"Don't drop it," he warned, swiftly moving towards her. The Ice Princess for some reason had totally lost her cool. "Hold on. I'll take it. Just don't *drop* it," he repeated the warning.

A visible shiver passed through her.

At least his tone was effective. "Let me have it."

He seemed to tower over her. *"David,"* she said, dismayed by the fact her normally composed voice was wavering.

His alternative name had never sounded so good, so intimate to his ears. He took the bowl from her, turning to place it on the rosewood library table that graced the entrance hall. "I startled you. I'm sorry." They were so close, barely a foot apart. He could see every little ripple along her throat as she swallowed. "Are you okay?' he asked. She appeared disorientated. This was a completely different Sonya from the one he had previously seen. Impossible as it seemed, she also looked frightened. Perhaps endangered was a better word?

Feeling very exposed, she tried to force herself back to attention. Her reaction had been a big mistake.

David, too, was feeling a degree of perturbation. His hand went to her sloping white shoulder. He meant only to steady her, but his fingers were bent on caressing her white skin, warm to his touch. This was no beautiful statue.

This was a living breathing woman. His eyes fell to the long heavy silk lock of her hair as it slid across his hand. He wanted to grasp a handful of it, pull her to him. He wanted to lower his head to capture her beautiful mouth that was surprisingly aquiver. He wanted to pick her up in his arms and carry her off like some caveman. Within seconds temptation after temptation was playing itself out. All common sense was getting away from him. This was mania. *Magic*, definitely black. She obviously had sirenlike powers. Fascinating men was a form of control. She could deliberately be luring him into her territory.

He stood back from her, the barriers springing back into place. "I'm sorry if I startled you. What are you doing here?" Given how he had *felt*, his voice sounded unnecessarily harsh. Was it guilt for slipping momentarily from his standards of behaviour?

For a moment she said nothing, giving her own protective shields a chance to get back into place. "Marcus has given me the job of doing the flowers for the house." She felt enormous relief some of her habitual cool composure had come back into her voice.

"I see. Where is Marcus?" he asked, looking down the spacious hallway with its beautiful parquetry floor towards the library. Marcus's favourite room.

"He's not here. But he should be home soon."

The way she spoke drove home the hurt. Did she think she could take Lucy's place? "I'll wait." The rush of sexual desire was replaced by hard distrust.

"Would you like a drink?" she asked, turning to lead him into the drawing room. "Coffee, something stronger?"

"I'm fine." He sounded just short of curt. "*You're* the one who looks like you could do with a stiff drink."

"You startled me, that's all."

"I might have been an intruder," he said, with more than a hint of sarcasm.

"Perhaps it was the quality of your own surprise," she returned. "You don't like or trust me." There was straight-forward challenge in her voice.

"It's not a question of liking, Ms Erickson. It's more to do with your *role*."

"Back to Ms Erickson, no Sonya?" She arched her fine brows.

"Sonya is a lovely name." He shrugged. "Tell me, is it your *real* name?"

"What an extraordinary question."

She had come to stand beneath a nineteenth century Russian chandelier, one of a matched pair in the yellow, gold and Wedgwood blue drawing room. In front of the white Carrara marble fireplace he noted she had placed a huge Chinese fish bowl filled with a wealth of sweet-smelling flowers. To add to the impact the beautiful pastel colours mimicked the colours in the magnificent nineteenth century Meissen porcelain clock that took centre place on the mantelpiece beneath a very valuable landscape. Other small arrangements were placed around the large room, rivalling the treasures on display.

"And?"

"Of course it's my real name," she said, one hand push-ing a thick lock of hair back off her shoulder.

The drawing room was all too feminine for his taste, too *opulent*, silks and brocades, but Sonya Erickson could have been made for it. Even in tight sexy jeans and designer vest-top she fitted in. It occurred to him with her hair worn long and loose and very little make-up she looked hardly more than a girl of nineteen or twenty.

He released a tense breath. "But what about the Erickson? Would you believe I actually knew a woman who changed her name four times? She's in jail now for fraud. She managed to extract the life savings from God knows how many fools of men."

"Please, don't make me weep!" she exclaimed. "Men *are* fools. But it's hardly fraudulent to change one's name by deed poll."

"Are you saying *you* have?'

She ignored his question. "Why don't you sit down?" she invited, with an elegant gesture of her hand.

"You might be in your own house," he answered, tightly. *Lucy's house.*

"Marcus has made me very welcome here." Her answer was equally pointed. "So you can't find out much about me. How disappointing for you. Is this what it's all about?"

"I came to see Marcus," he said. "I wasn't expecting *you*. Why don't you take the sofa?" he suggested. "I'll take the armchair. I know you're highly intelligent so we can cut to the chase. It's obvious my uncle has come to care deeply for you. And in a very short space of time. That presents problems, don't you agree?"

"Problems for *you*? I don't see the problem for me. Marcus is a lovely man. Was I supposed to submit my credentials to you? I might tell you Marcus has never asked anything of me. He trusts me."

His brilliant dark eyes flashed. "That's what I'm worried about. Who and what are you really, Sonya? What is it you want?"

"Who said I wanted anything?" she responded with an imperious lift of her brows. She took not the gold sofa, but a gilded armchair opposite him.

Sunlight was falling through the tall windows, filtered by the sheer central curtain. It illuminated her figure, making her hair and her beautiful skin radiant. "You were wearing

Aunt Lucy's diamond and emerald jewellery at the gala function," he said, the words freighted with meaning.

A flush like pink roses on snow warmed her cheeks. "Is there anything shameful about that? You're far too quick to place blame. Marcus *wanted* me to wear them. I could say insisted. He'd asked me the colour of my dress. When I said emerald green, he suggested a set of jewellery that needed an airing. I assure you the set is safely back in his safe."

It was too hard to resist. "Do you happen to know the combination?"

"Do *you*?" she shot back.

"I could open it blindfolded. I really don't want to offend you, Sonya."

"Then you couldn't be doing a better job," she said coldly, sitting very straight, long legs crossed neatly at the ankles.

Excellent deportment lessons there. "Your dress was exquisite, by the way. Did Marcus buy it for you?"

"Ah, the direct approach!" she said, looking down her finely cut nose at him. "I wore it because I had nothing better. Nor could I buy better. The dress is many years old."

He sat studying her. She appeared to be telling the truth.

"Vintage haute couture." She waved a hand.

"It looked it," he said, wanting to pierce her defences.

She shrugged a shoulder. "But you are not here to discuss my evening dress, which I might tell you belongs to me." She remembered her beautiful mother wearing it. But that was another time, another place, another world. A time when she had been happy.

"Actually I'm here to catch up with my uncle," he said,

breaking into her sad thoughts. "My love and loyalty is with him. You must understand that?"

She gave a light sceptical laugh. "Come now, you have no real right to interfere in his life, David. Marcus is a man in his fifties, a highly intelligent man."

"Who in all his adult years has never looked at another woman outside Lucy. Until now," he retorted sharply. "My big concern, Sonya, is that he doesn't get hurt. Extraordinarily enough Marcus is an innocent in his way. His health isn't all that good either. For years the whole family has been concerned he might simply die of a broken heart. That's how devoted he was to Lucy, his wife."

She flicked a platinum tendril off her heated cheek. "I understand the great pain of his loss. Marcus has told me many things about his beloved Lucy." She could tell him something of her own losses but her rigid sense of caution stopped her.

"Has he?" Another highly significant thing, he thought.

"Haven't you met anyone in your life you immediately identified with?" she asked, hostility in her beautiful green eyes.

He stared back at her, knowing he could never say he had identified with her. *On sight.*

"You won't be able to take Lucy's place, Sonya," he assured her. "No one will let you. You simply don't know what you're getting into. The Wainwright family is very powerful. You can't imagine how powerful. You wouldn't want to get them offside. You wouldn't want to embarrass them. *Family* is very important. So too is the Wainwright fortune. None of us would like to see a huge chunk of it going out of the family. We're all interconnected in business. You're far too young for Marcus. You know it. I know it. That said, many people would only see you in one way—as a woman on the make—and hate you for it."

"So what you're saying is, I couldn't possibly come up to your exalted standards?" she asked with surprisingly cool contempt. "Or is the fact Marcus is thirty years older the main objection?'

He showed his own anger. "If you were even twenty years older I doubt if I'd be saying any of this. You don't *love* Marcus, Sonya. Don't tell me you do."

"I wasn't about to tell you anything," she said icily. "The Wainwrights, who are they when it's all said and done? Billionaires? So what? That's not class, breeding, tradition. This nation is barely over two hundred years old. You're parvenus. Your English ancestor, Wainwright, only arrived in this country in the early eighteen hundreds, the flicker of an eyelid. Your family does *not* impress me."

"Evidently." He was somewhat taken aback by her remarks, yet amused. "So tell me about *your* illustrious family?" he challenged. "European aristocracy, were they? Counts and countesses a dime a dozen? Or haven't I given you sufficient time to get a really good story together? Maybe you're a fantasist? Where do you come from exactly? Is Erickson even your real name?"

"Maybe I change it," she said, sounding all of a sudden very foreign.

"Quite possible. My great-aunt Rowena thinks you have a slight Hungarian accent. She was married to a top British diplomat for many years. She knows Europe. She knows accents."

Her eyes blazed emerald. "Well, well, well! I can't find any other words."

"Surely it's not difficult for you to tell us something of your background? I'm ready to listen."

She stood up. "So sorry, David, but I'm not ready to

talk. Especially to *you*. You're very arrogant for so young a man."

He too rose to his feet, making her look small by comparison. "Beside you I'm an amateur," he said cuttingly.

Colour stained her high cheekbones. "You do not know the correct way to treat me."

"Or address you either. Should it be Contessa?" There was hard challenge in his strikingly handsome face.

"Who knows what might have been?" she said, then broke off abruptly, as if she had already volunteered too much. Her head tilted into a listening attitude. "That's Marcus now," she said thankfully, beginning to walk away from him. "I would not like him to find us arguing. Marcus is a very lonely man. He may think he's in love with me because I have green eyes. His Lucy had green eyes. I've no need to tell you that. Marcus loves you like his own son."

"So that gives me rights and obligations, doesn't it?" he answered tautly, tiring of her play-acting. "Lucy did have beautiful green eyes, but Lucy looked nothing like *you*. She didn't act like you either. She was a sweet, gentle woman, which by and large you *aren't*. What is it you're after?"

She turned to look at him with icy reserve. "I'm sorry, David. It seems to me that's none of your business. Now I must go and greet Marcus. You may not believe it, but I too want him to be happy."

He waited, resisting the urge to go to the window to witness the quality of the greeting. Moments later Marcus came into the living room, a spring in his step. He was looking better than he had looked for ages. There was colour in his skin, a brightness in his eyes. Marcus is a good man, he thought with a lunge of the heart. He deserves another chance at happiness. Only he wasn't going to stand by and allow a young woman who rebuffed any attempt to invade her privacy to damage their close loving relationship. What did she have to hide anyway? Ultimately her background would have to come out.

"David, I'm so glad you called in." Marcus bounded forward to seize his nephew's hand.

"I've missed seeing you," David responded. "Sonya has been looking after me."

"Wonderful. Wonderful!" Marcus enthused, drawing Sonya forward, his kind, distinguished face alight with pleasure. "I do so want you two to get to know each other better."

There was an unintended warning in that. He knew beyond doubt he had to forbid himself all and any erotic thoughts of Sonya Erickson. He couldn't possibly be the one to break his uncle's heart. On the other hand Ms Erickson, with all her barriers in place, would have to open up about her past.

Twenty minutes later Holt left. He had accepted one drink, Scotch over ice. He was driving and he was a guest at a dinner party that night. His emotions were in turmoil. He hadn't planned on any of this, but there was no avoiding the bitter truth now. Despite his very real concerns, he had become powerfully attracted to Sonya Erickson, if that was her real name. For the first time in his ordered life, he was losing his footing. No comfort to be drawn from that. The worst aspect was he knew he wouldn't give a damn who or what she was if she was the woman he wanted. She was in fact the *only* woman who had ever made such an impact on him. A different order altogether from his usual girlfriends. And there was Marcus looking better than he had looked in years. Marcus wanting he and Sonya to be *friends.*

God, what a mess!

If Sonya Erickson were truly in love with Marcus he would have to accept their marrying, whatever his private misgivings. But the beautiful Sonya, though obviously fond of Marcus—who could *not* be?—was *not* in love with him. Why was he so sure? Disturbing to know he could take her off Marcus whether she wanted it or not. Mutual attraction was very hard to hide. She was as attracted to him as he was to her. It hadn't crept up on them. In one of those sad ironies of life the attraction had been immediate. Neither had chosen the time. Now it was starting to take a heavy toll. Better they had never met. For an enigmatic young woman who presented herself as emotionally detached, what had drawn her to Marcus?

Apart from the money? said his cynical inner voice.

What had caused her to let down her guard? Marcus's essential goodness, his kindness, his courtly manner. More importantly Marcus would never pry. She had told him that herself. Did she want above anything a secure place in the world? Marcus could give her that. Did she fear being swept off her feet by some driving passion that could upset all her plans? She definitely had issues. Not a whole lot of trust in people. He'd already concluded it all had to do with her past life. Did a great need to be *safe* drive her? He was fast reaching the conclusion she was on the run from something. *Someone?* How would that impact on Marcus's plans?

There were too many question marks hanging over Ms Erickson's head. One thing was very clear. She was an extremely fast worker. She could be the second Mrs Marcus Wainwright if she so wanted. One heard of May/December marriages all the time. But in just about every case, the man was rich. He didn't like it. He didn't like it at all. He needed to talk to Rowena.

* * *

When he arrived at his apartment he rang Rowena to say he would be coming to Sunday lunch. Rowena always kept a marvellous table. More importantly, he and Rowena could keep an eye on proceedings and later confer.

"All right if I bring Paula?" he asked. "I know you're not fussed on her."

"Protection, dearest, is that it?"

He grimaced to himself. "I don't want to be seen to be using Paula. She'd actually love to be invited."

"Doesn't answer the question, dear."

"Marcus is madly in love with her, Rowena," he said firmly. "I was at the house this afternoon. Sonya was there, putting flowers all around the place."

"I bet they looked wonderful," Rowena's cultured voice fluted down the phone.

"She does have the genius touch. Did you know about this recent development?"

"Matter of fact I did. Sonia had some marvellous bromeliad stems for me. Wonderful to see with just a large green leaf hanging over the side."

"Rowena dear, I'm sure the bromeliads looked inspirational," he said edgily, "but what I most want to talk about is this. What is Sonya up to? She *knows* Marcus is in love with her. Can you really say with any degree of confidence a marriage between them might work, given the thirty-year leap? She could divorce him and get a hefty settlement. Break Marcus's heart. That's a huge worry."

"It's possible, my darling, but who is able to predict a marriage?"

"Now there's a cop out if ever there was one," he exclaimed. "She's won you over as well. You and Rolly had a great marriage. So do Mum and Dad."

"Ah, then, your mother had a great deal of money. So

did I. No one could ever have accused us of being fortune hunters. Makes things a lot easier."

"Mum is *four* years younger than Dad," he pointed out.

"My lovely Rolly was twelve years older than me."

"The perfect gentleman."

"He was indeed."

"You all brought a great deal to one another," he said. "What is Sonya going to bring to Marcus?"

Rowena chuckled. Over-long.

"Okay, okay, but is she in it for short term gain, Rowena? I'd love to look on the positive side, but I couldn't bear to see Marcus humiliated. She doesn't love him. That's the pity. But she does have him wrapped around her little finger. He's happy at the moment. Really happy. I have to say it's lovely to see."

Rowena abruptly sobered. "I'm as concerned as you are, David. For both of them. You know, dear, I've come to the conclusion Sonya is carrying a burden she can't lay down. Despite that poise of hers, the high-born air, she seems to me a little lost."

"Lost?" For a moment he thought he might lose it entirely. "She's as switched on as they come."

"Lighten up, love," Rowena advised. "I know how much you love Marcus. You've always looked up to him. You have heart. You're also very perceptive. I do realize the developing situation had to be taken very seriously. I'm with you there. Marcus, up until he met Sonya, has acted as though all happiness had passed him by."

"It's a dilemma, isn't it?" he said. "Marcus is the one who stands to be hurt. Even if a marriage did take place, marriages end. A beautiful young woman with a large settlement could move on. Marcus would not. We both know that."

"Yes indeed," Rowena quietly agreed.

"We can expect fireworks from Dad and Mum. Dad especially. He loves his brother. Dad will want Sonya thoroughly checked out. Even then he wouldn't approve. Neither would Mum. You know what they're like. You know what the family is like. They'll condemn her right off as a fortune hunter and a fake."

"Well, she's not faking the patrician air," Rowena said in strong defence of the young woman she had come to like and admire.

"She's a mystery woman indeed," David answered, very, very dryly.

"There's a story there, my darling. But not a happy one, I'm sure."

"It makes a lot of women happy marrying a millionaire," he pointed out.

"In a lot of cases it doesn't work out marrying for love," she countered. "I hear the Grantleys are divorcing. How long ago was it we were at the wedding?"

"Not long enough for them to open the wedding presents," he said. "So, see you Sunday."

"Looking forward to it."

Problems. Problems. Problems, Rowena thought as she hung up.

Was it possible beautiful young Sonya was in some way flawed? Had she a plan in mind? Marcus could offer her the good life, but would she be content for long with that? And what did Sonya think of David? She felt deeply troubled now. David was a marvellous young man. She couldn't count the number of women young and old who had succumbed to David's extraordinary charm. David had everything going for him. Sonya would be a rare woman if she didn't feel his attraction. So what *did* Sonya think of David? On Sunday she would make it her business to find out.

CHAPTER THREE

What am I doing? Where am I going with my life? I was coping well enough. Now I feel utter confusion.

She often got caught up in conversations with herself. Sonya sat in front of her mirror while she put in her earrings. These days all she could seem to focus on was David Wainwright and the mounting tensions and difficulties springing up between them. She wanted to stop thinking about him, but his image was so compelling he broke again and again into her consciousness, no matter how hard she tried to keep up the barricades. She had the dismal feeling her past life with its tragedies had damaged her. Well, she was damaged, she admitted, but *for ever*? That was a frightening prognosis.

Maintain the distance. Maintain the emotional barriers. You need no more complications in life.

There was no getting away from the voice in her head. Everyone had one, but, her being so much alone in life since the tender age of sixteen, her inner voice only got stronger. David Wainwright's mental image was so persistent, so vivid, for the first time in her life she understood how dangerous powerful sexual attraction could be. It played havoc with one's control. And he was coming to Lady Palmerston's buffet lunch!

You'll be seeing him again! Oh, sweet Lord! Forget the man.

Only her senses were exquisitely, excruciatingly sharpened. She realized to her dismay it was affecting her normal behaviour. Only how did one stop the mix of excitement and panic that stormed through her? She needed to block both emotions. A woman's weakness only gave a man power. She didn't want any man to dominate her thoughts, let alone her life. She wanted peace, peace, *peace.* A mature man, who had suffered himself, could give her that. Peace was important, a sense of being protected. God knew she'd had little of it in her fraught life. At twenty-five, she was still in recovery. At least that was how she thought of it.

Recovery.

Her history was a tragic one. But no one must know it. Not yet. When it came down to it meeting the Wainwrights had only complicated her life. She had to decide what she needed to do next. In less than half an hour, Marcus would be picking her up in his chauffeured Bentley. Marcus was a true gentleman, noble of character, much as her father had been. It would be a sin to lead Marcus on yet she knew she could have a real life with Marcus. No dramas. No concealing her true identity. She would have security. The age difference didn't really bother her. Or it hadn't until she had met Marcus's nephew, David. Waves of emotion started to wash over her…

God, if you're up there, you have to help me! I've no one else to call on.

Her parents had died very tragically in a car crash, ten years before. Only the crash had been engineered. She knew by whom. He would never do it himself. He would never be brought to justice. He lived in far-off America. But he had the power, the connections and the money to organize a hit even across continents. There would never be a mention of his name in connection with the tragic event. Laszlo had many friends in high places, even if he had many more enemies. But they couldn't get to him. Like the Wainwrights, Laszlo was a billionaire with huge international interests in oil and steel.

And she had something he wanted very badly. The Andrassy Madonna. A precious icon that had been in the family since the seventeenth century. Up until recent times Laszlo had believed the Madonna, fashioned by medieval craftsmen—her robes and headpiece studded with diamonds, rubies, emeralds and seed pearls—had disappeared into the hands of the invading Russians when the estate was pillaged at the end of the Second World War. Laszlo's father, Karoly, had done the wise thing gathering up his family and what he could of his fortune and fleeing Europe for the United States and safety. There, he became enormously rich again.

Her great-grandfather had stayed to the death. His eldest son, Matthias, the heir, had elected to stay with his father, resisting all pleas to make his escape. It was her grandmother, Katalin, who, as a little girl, had been the one to escape with the help of a loyal family servant. Her great-grandfather and her great-uncle had been taken prisoners and never seen or heard of again. It was a tragic story repeated all over war-torn Europe and Russia.

But the Madonna believed to be lost for ever was in her possession. Proof of her identity. It gave her power, but offered no immunity against Laszlo. Rather the reverse. Possession put her in danger. After the Berlin Wall came down the estate had been returned to the Andrassy-Von Neumann family, albeit in ruins. Laszlo claimed to be the rightful heir and gained possession of the estate, when she was the rightful heir. Only she would never make her claim. Never be in a position to make it. Laszlo would get rid of her before he allowed her to take anything he considered belonged to him. She would be just another young woman to go missing never to be seen again. Laszlo was a powerful man with all the money and a team of lawyers. She had neither. She had long since learned Might was Right. Not the other way around. Laszlo had been pumping a great deal of money into the country of his birth, buying influence and friends in high places. Many of the valuable stolen paintings and artifacts had been returned to him, but the thing Laszlo most wanted was the Andrassy Madonna.

And she had it. The *one* thing her grandmother had been able to spirit out of a war-torn Hungary.

She shook herself out of her dark, disturbing memories. For a short but intense period of her life, she had found herself in enemy territory, struggling to get by with no one close to trust. The risks had been compounded by her sex. A good-looking young girl on her own was considered fair game. Here in this country of such peace and freedom she was getting herself together. She regretted some of the things she had said to David Wainwright, especially the bit about his family being parvenus. One of her tempestuous moments. She'd thought she had learned to override them, but contact with David only made her painfully aware the wide range of emotions of her preadolescent years, when she had such wonderful parental care, were reforming.

For the occasion she had mixed two pieces she liked and felt confident in: a lovely apricot silk shirt with the sleeves pushed up, tucked into a great pair of cream silk-cotton trousers. She had settled on a wide deep pink and cream leather belt to sling around her waist. The belt pulled the outfit together. Several long dangly necklaces, pretty but inexpensive, around her neck, a striking silk scarf patterned in apricot, pink and chocolate, to tie back her long hair at the nape. She had a good cream leather shoulder bag to go with the outfit. The latest in high-heeled sandals. She knew Paula Rowlands would be there. If the Valentino David's girlfriend had worn at the gala was anything to go on she knew how to dress. She wondered how serious the relationship might be. It wasn't intense or she would have noticed. But money married money. Everyone knew that. Passion waned. Money handled wisely just grew and grew.

Lady Palmerston's residence was situated in the most elite location in the entire country, nestling as it did between beautiful blue bays with breathtaking views of the Harbour Bridge and the Opera House. Marcus had told her on the drive over David had a penthouse apartment less than five minutes away. Maybe he often walked over to visit his great aunt. She realized if one had to enquire how much properties like these were worth, one didn't have and would never have the money to afford them. Now she had an extremely wealthy man as a good friend. She knew she could make something come of it. A lot of women regarded marrying a rich man as a goal in life. Could she? She and Marcus were moving inexorably into another stage of their relationship. Falling in love with his nephew was *unthinkable*.

Yet her grandmother had been born in a palace. No fantasy, the truth. Sonya had never dared visit the magnificent Andrassy-Von Neumann estate but she had been shown many old books and seen the photographs of it taken before the Second World War broke out in Europe. She had studied them over and over, awestruck. Her grandmother had been born in a fairy-tale palace? The palace looked like something out of a dream. But the dream had been destroyed. She knew the estate had been taken over by the advancing Russian army in 1945. The stately palace had been left a wreck and its great tracts of valley with its lake, trees and wonderful gardens and glorious statuary left in ruin and rubble. All of the statues of gods and goddesses, water nymphs and the like had been used for target practice. Many act of senseless revenge, the glass in all the windows smashed. Inside the great house the grand collections of family crystal, glass and handmade porcelains. The valuable paintings had been declared sacrosanct. They had been carefully wrapped up and taken away.

War.

Was there ever going to be an end to it? She thought, *Never.* Life took some momentous turns. There were countless stories of reversals of fortune down through the ages. The Czar and his family who had lived in splendour had died in horrifying circumstances. The last Emperor of China had lived out his life as a market gardener. Her beautiful dispossessed grandmother had died relatively early, with a broken heart that had never mended. Her mother, taught both Hungarian and German at her mother's knee, had sailed through her days like a swan on a lake, with perfect composure, but it was a composure that masked her deep, deep grief.

She had told Marcus none of this. Marcus didn't even know her real name. As she had told David, Marcus didn't pry. She knew he was waiting for her to confide in him, but she had built such walls of defence. Talking about her past would be accompanied by an inrush of pain. No one need know her traumas. All these long years no one outside her grandmother, her parents, now herself had laid eyes on the Madonna. She had not been allowed to see the Madonna herself until her sixteenth birthday. That had been two short weeks before her parents had been so cruelly killed.

Always remember Laszlo is out there to do you harm.

Memories of her mother's green eyes looking into hers,

her mother's patrician hand stroking her long blonde hair. Good blood was in the genes.

The man past his first youth who wanted her had given her the news of their death, trying to take her into his arms, but she had resisted wildly, even so young recognising the erotic undercurrent in the family relationship. It was a terrifying thing to be left so powerless. She had waited and planned. Then she had disappeared. From that moment on always on the run. It was the equivalent of being turned out on the streets.

The buffet tables set up in the air-conditioned indoors were draped in spotless white linen, and laden with delectable food. In passing Sonya saw whole seared salmons, ocean trout, stacks of oysters, prawns galore, sea scallops, lobsters and delicious little "bugs". There was also carved grain-fed lamb for those who liked a mix; warm salads, cold salads, potato salads, all the accompaniments. It could feed a Third World country.

The guest list was for a party of twenty. Four large glass-topped rectangular tables shaded by royal blue, white-fringed umbrellas were in place for al fresco dining. One could choose indoors or out, though the informal living room with its white marble floor and largely white furnishings was open to the broad terrace with its white canopy by way of a series of foldaway glass doors that brought the spectacular view in.

They were greeted warmly by Rowena, who led them out onto a sun-drenched terrace where the guests who had already arrived were assembled enjoying a glass of whatever they fancied, served by two handsome young man in jaunty uniforms that featured very dashing waist-length fitted jackets. Sonya recognised the logo of the excellent catering company Rowena had employed. She herself had provided the wealth of prize blooms, including some exquisite lotus blossoms, along with a generous amount of assorted leaves for Lady Palmerston to arrange herself. Lady Palmerston was as passionate about flowers as she was.

Smiles on all sides. Warm hellos. Nice to meet you. Some of the older ladies she knew. They were now her clients, thanks to their hostess. Mercifully Paula Rowlands's antagonism wasn't on display. Not yet anyway. Though Paula soon turned back to resume her conversation with her own kind of people.

Sonya watched as David Wainwright hugged his uncle. They were very close. There was no one to hug her like that any more. No family who had been out to look after her, just exploit her. When the moment came, David Wainwright all but shocked her by bending his handsome dark head to lightly brush her cheek. A couple of seconds only, yet she felt the thrill of it right down to her toes. When she looked up, his brilliant glance was hooded. It was obvious he wanted only happiness for his uncle, and just as obvious he didn't see her as any sort of a solution.

Marcus had been drawn away for a moment by two of his old chums, Dominic and Elizabeth Penry-Evans, one a Supreme Court judge, the wife an eminent barrister. David turned to her, his tone friendly, but laced with challenge. "How nice to see you here, Sonya."

"Very pleased to be here, David." She gave him a cool little smile. No need for him to know she was trying to slow her quickened breath. "This has to be one of the most glorious views on earth," she said, looking across the turquoise swimming pool to the sparkling blue harbour with its view of the famous Coat Hanger, the Sydney Harbour Bridge, and the world famous Opera House with its glittering white sails. "I believe you live only a short distance away?"

He was wrestling with an overpowering urge to pull at the silk scarf that tied back her beautiful hair. He wanted to see it loose and blowing, cascading around her face and over her shoulders. It was wonderful hair. "No doubt you will see my apartment some time," he said, adopting a careless tone.

"No urgency." She remained looking out over the spectacular view.

"I don't actually know where *you* live," he said. "But we can't forget you're something of a mystery woman."

She turned back, lifting her chin.

It was an amazingly imperious gesture, he thought. A simple lift of the chin? Who *was* this woman? One thing was certain: she had gone to great lengths to hide her background.

"Of course you do," she said. "It's a wonder I haven't stumbled over one of your spies."

He gave her a twisted smile. "Maybe spying is a very harsh word. Just a little checking."

"So you know I don't live in your part of town." The air around them seemed to be vibrating like the beating wings of a hummingbird.

"Well, maybe down a notch," he said lightly.

"How kind."

"You do admit to a chip on your shoulder, Sonya?" He knew he should move away from her. Only he couldn't. He really *couldn't*. He saw it as a blow to his self-control.

"I admit to a chip on *both* shoulders," she responded with mocking sweetness. "But it has nothing to do with not having a lot of money, or not moving in your illustrious circles, David."

How good his name on her lips sounded. No one else said it the same way. He got Holt from his mother. She *was* a Holt and never let anyone forget it. "Surely there's a strong possibility that's all going to change?"

"You'll be the first to know, David," she said scathingly.

"Marcus is already in love with you. But it's not *you*, Sonya, I'm worried about. You're obviously a young woman who knows how to look after herself."

Her emerald eyes flashed like jewels in the sunlight. "Is that so strange? Women have had to fight long and hard for independence, recognition. And the fight isn't over."

"And you've had to fight very hard to be strong?" It could explain so much about her.

"What woman doesn't?" she said scornfully, clearly on the defensive.

"Why so hostile, Sonya?" he asked. "Has some man really hurt you?" He found he badly wanted to know. She had presented her lovely profile so he couldn't look into her eyes. He had to face the fact he had an ever-growing need to discover all there was to know about this young woman.

For Marcus, or for yourself?

He felt shamed by the thought. For God's sake, she was here with Marcus.

"I have met threatening, difficult and a few terrifying men," she said, almost tonelessly. "Does that answer your question? I dare say there would be many women who could say the same. Battered, abused women who never saw it coming. I feel truly secure with Marcus."

His brows knotted in a frown. "And the feeling of security needs to be locked into your relationships?"

"Exactly." She stood motionless, her head turned away from him.

"So in a different situation where you could fall madly in love you would regard yourself as being under threat?"

She was startled by how he had hit on a problematic area. Her lack of trust in men. "Falling in love is a kind of madness, surely?" she parried. "Who can say being madly in love is essential to a good marriage? There are other very worthwhile things. So why don't you let Marcus worry about himself, David? He's a grown man. Or is it the *money*? Are you his heir?"

"Careful, Sonya," he warned.

"Touched a raw nerve, have I?" She turned back to him then, her beautiful eyes frankly mocking.

"If you're looking for raw nerves, you haven't found it," he said curtly. He was in fact the main beneficiary of Marcus's will.

"But then you're a man who doesn't get frazzled easily," she said. "But it's not nonsense entirely. It's often said, no one can have too much money."

"It's also said money can't guarantee happiness." He cut her off tersely.

"Maybe not, but it can guarantee wonderful houses to live in, superb views." She waved an elegant hand. "The best cars, yachts." Wonderful yachts with billowing sails were out on the sparkling blue water. "I'm told you're a fine yachtsman. Then there are clothes, jewels. You name it. Everything pretty well comes down to money."

"And you want it?"

"What I want is a pleasant day," she retorted, ultra cool.

"Of course you do," he said suavely. "I apologise. You must be pleased your fame with flowers has spread far and wide. Liz over there with Marcus has been into your shop. Two of Rowena's friends now present. Rowena, of course. She told me you provided all the very beautiful flowers for today?"

It was too much not to look at him. She felt compelled.

He was wearing a dark blue and white striped casual shirt of best quality cotton, beautifully cut white linen trousers, navy loafers on his feet. His polished skin was tanned to bronze, against which his fine teeth showed very white. He could have posed for a Ralph Lauren shoot, she thought wryly. "I've worked hard to secure the best sources," she said, with a touch of pride.

"I expect Paula will be next to pay you a visit." It was a taunt really. Unworthy of him.

"Please God, *no*!" she said with a charming little gesture of her hands.

"Hello? Does this mean you don't like her?"

"Do *you*?" She shot him a glance as cool and clear as crystal.

His expression turned sardonic. "I've adored her since childhood."

"Then clearly I've overestimated you."

He couldn't help it. He laughed aloud.

It was such an engaging laugh it caused the guests to look in their direction to smile. David Wainwright was a great favourite.

"That's very naughty of you, Sonya. And you the Ice Princess."

"I never said I was a nice person," she countered, not lightly, but with a hint of warning.

"Maybe I bring out the worst in you?" he asked. Her skin in the bright sunlight was as flawless as a baby's. One could become enslaved by a woman like this. He would do well to heed the warning.

"Well, you do give it your best shot." She paused, her tone changing. "Your girlfriend is on the way over."

He didn't turn his head. "I don't remember saying Paula was my girlfriend."

"I don't remember saying Marcus was my man friend," she returned sharply.

Paula Rowlands was not so much strolling as striding up to them. No doubt she was fuelled by the feline need to protect her territory, Sonya thought. "Here she comes. Hostility writ large upon her face. It must have been triggered by your laughing. It sounded too much like you were enjoying yourself."

He let his eyes run over her. "Actually, Sonya, I *was*."

Throughout the leisurely meal Rowena asked them to shift to different tables so everyone got an opportunity to speak to all the other guests. Sonya found herself having a delightful time. She had come prepared for undercover distrust; instead she might have been among friends. Of course she wasn't obviously paired with Marcus. On the contrary she was treated as a free spirit. That was exactly what she wanted. Every time she sat at table with David Wainwright every nerve in her body flared into life. It was as if she were made of highly flammable tissue paper and his nearness set her alight.

A very pretty, chic young woman called Camilla Carstairs was especially friendly. They arranged to meet up for coffee midweek. Camilla promised to come into the shop. "I've heard so much about it, Sonya. The flowers today are amazingly beautiful." Sonya found herself warming to such friendliness. She found out later, Camilla was the only daughter of "Mack" Carstairs, the trucking king.

After lunch the older couples retired to the house, while the younger guests remained outside or took strolls around the landscaped garden, an oasis of beauty and peace. A few ventured down to the turquoise swimming pool at the harbour's edge. Though Sonya had been seated at times with Paula Rowlands, Paula had had very little to say to her. Now Paula intended to change all that. She detached herself from a small group that did not include David Wainwright. He appeared to have gone inside. Meanwhile Paula made a beeline for Sonya, calling out her name.

"Yoo-hoo, Sonya, wait for me." She waved enthusiastically.

Here comes trouble, said the voice in Sonya's head.

And it wasn't wrong.

Paula, the very picture of friendliness, linked her arm through Sonya's as though they were bosom pals. Immediately it put Sonya back on guard.

"When did *this* happen?" she asked lightly, resisting the urge to pull away.

"What happen?" Paula widened her eyes.

"A big turnaround comes to mind." Sonya smiled.

Paula gave a laugh that was not reflected in her eyes. "Walk on with me," she said. "I *need* to talk to you."

"Sounds a bit like you need something to calm you more," Sonya offered wryly. She was well aware of Paula's seething jealousy.

"Ah, the little witticisms!" Paula tried to pull Sonya along.

Stand still. You could be looking at pandemonium here.

Sonya obeyed her inner voice. "I really think you can say whatever it is you want to say right here, Paula." The blue glitter of the water was all around them. A fairly strong breeze was blowing in, whipping at Sonya's silk scarf. "Is something the matter?"

Paula pealed another laugh. There they were, the two of them enjoying a jolly time. "You're becoming too friendly with Holt." Paula came right to the point, her voice pitched low, but her eyes brimming with strong emotion. "I'll go a step further. I believe you're deliberately trying to take him off me."

Some imp of mischief made her say, "I wish!" Unwise.

"Then you *are*?" Paula showed her outrage.

"I'm joking, Paula. Just a little joke." Sonya backed off. "Look, why don't you speak to David about your concerns?"

"David? *David*!" Paula sounded almost violent. "His name is Holt."

"Surely that's a nickname he was given as a child?" Sonya said. "I like David better."

"*You* like!" Paula's voice had turned into a croak. "Most people call him Holt. His mother is—"

"I know, the Holt heiress." Sonya nodded calmly. "I suppose if I did a quick whip around I'd find you're all staggeringly rich."

"Indeed we are!" Paula's face registered contempt. "And you the florist!"

"Is that meant to downgrade me? You merely sound a snob. I'm a very good florist as it happens. You can order over the phone. In fact, if you're looking for work in very pleasant surroundings, I might be able to put some your way. I understand you don't have a job." She was beyond anger. She just wanted to get away from this jealous young woman.

It took a decided wrench to get her arm back, though she tried not to make it obvious to anyone who might be watching. Her back to the pool, she didn't realize she was now standing too close to the edge. Paula kept her eyes so fixed on her, she might have been attempting hypnosis.

"The big difference between you and me, Ms Erickson, is I don't have to work. You envy me. I know you do. I can't blame you. I've got everything you want. Everything you'll never get." She spoke quite threateningly. "Remember, I'm watching you."

From long practice, Sonya was able to keep a rein on her own temper. "Do you suppose that bothers me?" she asked coolly.

Colour mottled Paula's cheeks. "It should! I'm in a position to make things go rather badly for you."

"I'm supposed to take that as a threat?"

"Take it any way you like," Paula said sharply. "Doesn't it make you happy you've got poor old Marcus wrapped around your little finger?"

"Happy? It makes me ecstatic." Sonya felt reduced to black humour. "Is *that* want you want to hear?"

Paula sucked in her breath, looking aghast. "So you admit it! I think it's absolutely loathsome what you're doing. You're nothing but a gold-digger."

"You should stop listening to gossip, Paula. And might I remind you I'm a guest here, just like you." How did she get rid of this woman? She was fully aware she was looking into the face of raw jealousy. Jealousy was a malignancy. It ate into the soul. "Do you think we might call a truce here and now, Paula?" she suggested, in a conciliatory voice. "You surely can't want a scene? You'll be upsetting Lady Palmerston."

"Like you're *not*?" Paula challenged, fiercely affronted by the suggestion they were equals. "Rowena and Holt are right onto you. That's why you've been invited. So they can keep an eye on you. Holt told me. He tells me everything. We all know who's doing the upsetting." Paula stepped nearer. Oddly there was a smile on her face.

A warning should have lit up like a neon sign. Sonya knew in an instant she had backed up dangerously close to the edge of the pool. But the speed with which she pitched backwards into the water stunned her. Gulps of it went down her throat. The pool water was surprisingly cold, to her shocked body near *freezing*. It closed over her head, locking her in its shining blue depths. The impact drained her whole body of strength. Panic flooded into her brain. She was flailing helplessly.

Her inner voice kicked in, giving her orders.

Lift up your arms. Kick your legs. Stroke upwards. Come on. You can do it.

She felt her sandals slide off her feet. Her clothes, even her long hair, were holding her down. With a huge effort she shot to the surface, water streaming off her head. She had time to catch an agonised half-breath, then she went down again, her heart pounding. This time she had the sense to clamp her mouth shut.

The embarrassing part was, she couldn't swim. How humiliating was that? She had never learned like any four-year-old Australian child how to swim.

Poolside, Paula, in tears now, was screaming for help. Sonya could hear the scream reverberating underwater. Paula hadn't pushed her. Paula hadn't touched her. Paula had simply manoeuvred her nearer the edge. Her high heels and loss of balance had done the rest. She couldn't possibly drown. There were too many people around. Anyone who said the drowning process was euphoric had it all wrong.

Next thing she knew a solid body was in the water with her. A strong arm arced out and grabbed her. The arm easily reeled her in. She clung to her rescuer, barely seeing him with the water in her eyes. But she knew who it was even before their heads hit the surface.

David.

Her chin was at water level.

"Spit it out. Spit the water out," he ordered, gripping her tight. "It's okay. I've got you."

She did as she was told.

"Good girl. You'll be fine now."

"Oh, my God!" She couldn't help herself. She moaned. Other guests crossed her vision. All wore anxious faces. No one was laughing.

"It's all right, Sonya," David assured her. "You can't swim?"

Instead of answering his question she found herself saying quite tartly, "I wasn't planning on going in the water."

His smile flashed. "Good. You sound more like yourself."

A young man called Raymond, who had been very attentive to Sonya during the afternoon, crouched over, reaching out an arm. "I'll take her from here, Holt."

"Thanks, Ray."

While Raymond and another young man hauled Sonya out of the water, Holt dived to the bottom of the pool to retrieve Sonya's high-heeled sandals. Then when he surfaced he passed them to a distressed Rowena while he heaved himself out. He had rid himself of his own shoes before taking his unscheduled dive.

Rowena and Marcus were on hand, both looking upset, holding up towelling robes. One pink. One navy. "Here, dear girl, put this on," Rowena urged, holding out the pink robe with such kindness tears sprang to Sonya's eyes. Marcus was busy helping his nephew into the navy robe, which David used to towel over his water-sleeked dark head.

"Come into the house," Rowena bid Sonya quietly. "We'll get you dry."

Sonya began apologizing. "I'm so sorry for spoiling such a lovely day, Lady Palmerston. I was standing too near the edge. I slipped. I can't swim unfortunately."

"I'll teach you," Ray called out with enthusiasm. Even

sopping, Sonya looked *glorious*. A real erotic turn-on. The silk shirt was plastered to her high breasts, revealing peaked nipples and darkish pink aureole.

"Poor old you!" Camilla moved in closer to rub Sonya's back consolingly. "But look at it this way. You're not the first person to take an unexpected header into that pool. Paula should have known better. Where is she anyway?" Camilla turned her glossy head.

"I expect she's upset," Sonya heard herself saying, modestly pulling her soaked shirt away from her breasts.

"Like we all care!" Camilla whispered in Sonya's ear. "Want me to come with you?"

Sonya tried a smile. "Thanks, Camilla, but I'll be fine once I'm out of these wet things."

Inside the house Marcus studied Sonya very intently. "I do so wish that hadn't happened to you, my dear. You slipped?"

He appeared so shaken, Sonya reached out a gentle hand to stroke his cheek. "A silly accident, Marcus. Not to worry."

"I wish I could believe that." His distinguished face looked decidedly unhappy.

"It was an accident, Marcus," she stressed, painfully aware she was dripping pool water all over the floor. "Let it go."

Marcus glanced over to where Rowena, head bent, was having a few quiet words with David. "I'll get you home," Marcus said.

"But you've been so enjoying yourself," she protested. "It's been a lovely afternoon. I like to see you so relaxed. You would have to call your chauffeur back."

Marcus shook his head. "That's not a problem. It's his job."

Rowena walked quickly over to them. "I've suggested to David he take you home, Sonya. He wants to go now. He'll take you if you're happy with that?"

David too moved back towards them, addressing his uncle. "It's no problem, Marcus, to drop Sonya off. I expect, like me, she wants to go. Your chauffeur will take a good thirty minutes to make the return journey. Rowena would like you to stay on a while longer."

Sonya began to finger comb her long wet hair. "Yes, please stay, Marcus," she urged, though Marcus looked most undecided. "The last thing I want is for a silly accident to ruin your day. I'll ring you this evening. Promise."

"*Please*," Marcus answered.

So it was arranged.

CHAPTER FOUR

THEY were out on the open road, the big car moving soundlessly except for the soft purr of the air conditioning. Neither of them had said anything for a full five minutes but all sorts of sparks were flying, each trying to envision what was on the other's mind. Sonya was wearing a brand-new pink tracksuit Lady Palmerston had provided her with. David's tracksuit was pearl grey. Obviously outfits like theirs were kept on hand for guests.

"I have an idea that wasn't an accident." David was the one to break the silence, his expression on the grim side. He had seen through Paula's Academy-Award-winning performance.

Sonya shook her head. Her hair was billowing madly from the dip in the pool water, but it was almost dry after a few minutes with a hairdryer. Lady Palmerston's Filipina maid, Maria, had attended her, taking charge of her wet clothes, except for her bra and briefs, which had been popped in the dryer so she could put them back on. "Entirely my fault," she said.

"Camilla told me you were standing with Paula."

"You can safely rule out any push." She had seen the accusation in Camilla's eyes, heard it in her voice, so it wasn't difficult to guess what Camilla had told him.

"Can I now?" he asked, tersely shooting a quick glance at her.

"What happened to Paula anyway? Surely you didn't leave her behind?"

"Paula came in her own car. She went home in it too. Very upset, or so she made it appear."

"Poor Paula!" she dryly commiserated.

"Give me a break!" he retorted. "Paula pushed you."

"Paula never laid a finger on me," she said firmly. "Though I certainly didn't make that spectacular jump on purpose. Paula and I had a few words. It made me less cautious around the pool."

"So, then, it was a planned manoeuvre?"

"I never said that at all."

"You're being very gracious," he offered.

"It comes very easily to me."

"Those aristocratic genes for sure," he pointed out sardonically. "Anyway, I must apologize."

She half smiled. "I enjoy hearing you apologize."

"I thought you might. What were you talking about anyway?"

She stared through the window at the beautiful day. People were out and about in their numbers, enjoying the sunshine and their naturally beautiful city with its magnificent blue harbour. They were passing a small park, a lovely sanctuary of mature shade trees and broad stretches of lush green grass. Children were playing around a central fountain, others had claimed the swings, attended by their doting parents. One little girl in a pretty dress patterned with delicate wildflowers waved joyfully at her. Sonya waved back, a tender smile on her face.

"*You*, would you believe?" she said and gave a faint laugh.

He groaned, shooting her another quick glance. She looked ravishing with her white-gold mane draped like luminous curtains around her face and falling down her back. The pink of the tracksuit was perfect against her white skin. "So are you going to tell me?"

"No."

He responded with a crooked smile. "If I say please?"

She shook her head. "You don't *need* to know. But I will tell you this. She believes I'm a *gold-digger*. Her words, echoing yours."

"A woman as beautiful as you doesn't have to do a damn thing. Much less dig," he said crisply. "Marcus is one thing. But why would *I* come into the conversation?"

"My dear David," she answered with supreme nonchalance, "the woman would *kill* for you."

"I assume you're joking?" There was a decided edge to his voice.

"You should have a word with her," she suggested. "It's not every day a girl has *two* Wainwrights to choose from. She said I was—wait for it—after *you* as well!"

"She *didn't*." He almost cringed. It was up to him now to put Paula straight. It hadn't worked before. It would now.

"Paula is suffering," Sonya pointed out, not without empathy. "If you don't love her, maybe you should put her out of her misery? Or is it the mother you're worried about? I understand she's the mother from hell."

He laughed. "Who told you that?"

"As if I'd reveal my sources!"

"Raymond." He hit on the answer. "Did he ask for your phone number?"

"He's coming into the shop. He's very attractive. I liked him."

"He obviously *loved* you." His tone was openly goading.

"Isn't that sweet? I'm so enjoying mixing with the mega-rich."

He slotted the Mercedes smoothly between two little run-abouts. "This will give the neighbours something to talk about," she said.

"Aren't you going to ask me up?" He turned his handsome face to her.

"I dare not," she said sharply.

He gave her a smile that would make the strongest-willed woman go weak at the knees. "Oh, come on, Sonya. Do you get many visitors?"

"Not too many."

"At the very least you can make me a cup of coffee. I want to see where you live."

"You *know* where I live," she said, in an off-putting tone. "In fact you never even asked for directions."

"Let's get out," he suggested.

"If you must."

The voice of caution kicked in. *This is going to be very, very tricky.*

The apartment complex wasn't the top end of the market, or anywhere near it, but it was attractive, a contemporary design, well maintained, and in a quiet suburban street. There were only four floors. Sonya's apartment was at the top. There was no one in the lift. Sonya didn't look at him on the way up. She was worryingly off balance, but determined to hide it. She knew if he touched her—even her hand—everything would change. So he must *not* touch her. And she couldn't afford to be too friendly. Her involuntary physical reactions to him were depleting her supply of self-control. There could be no winners here. Not him.

Certainly not her. For her there would be punishment of some kind.

They were inside the small two-bed apartment. Sonya had filled it with the sort of things that reminded her of her early life.

Holt looked around with pleasure. "You decorated this yourself?" He had already guessed the answer. "Where did you get all the old pieces?"

She watched in some wonderment as he moved around the living room. David Wainwright *here*! She almost felt like bursting into emotional tears. She had been so *lonely*. Marcus, lovely man that he was, couldn't hope to fill the sad void in her. *But David!* She berated herself for her weakness. "I picked them up from demolition yards, jumble sales, second-hand shops." She managed to sound perfectly calm. "It's amazing what people part with. I had to work on all my finds, of course. I love timber."

"So do I. This appeals to me greatly." He ran a hand over the back of a carved chair with very fine finials. It looked Russian.

"I'm absolutely delighted." She purposely spiked her tone.

Keep it light. Don't deepen the connection.

The living-dining area was the usual open plan, he saw. There was a galley-like small kitchen with granite bench tops and good stainless-steel appliances. The balcony had been made a relaxing green haven with luxuriant plants. But what she had done to an ordinary space was what impressed him.

"This has a lot of character." A beautiful scrap of tapestry had been used to cover the top of the cushion on its seat. "Not *our* sort of character where the emphasis is generally on exploiting the natural light, the sunshine and the indoor-outdoor lifestyle. This is a glimpse into a different world.

Neo-Gothic maybe?" He glanced across the room at her, his eyes touching on her face and lissom body.

"There's that," she agreed. "I like the way the timbers gleam so darkly against the white walls. The white-tiled floor I managed to cover with a really good rug, as you can see. That set me back a bit but it was worth it. I don't own the apartment. I rent it."

"And the big painting on the wall?" His interest was truly captured.

"Mine," she said. "Anyone can paint flowers."

"No, they *can't*!" He moved nearer the painting, an oil reminiscent of the Dutch school: dark background, lightly touched with green and mauve strokes, with massed flower heads, roses, peonies, lilies, others, taking up the entire central canvas. "This is very painterly," he said with genuine admiration.

"I can't resist flowers. I used a palette knife."

"Aren't you clever!" He was giving the painting his full attention. "Who taught you?"

"Oh, a relative," she said evasively.

"As forthcoming as usual?" His black eyes mocked. "You know, you could make a good living as an artist, Sonya. I could help you."

"You think that preferable to my capturing your uncle's heart and along the way a good slice of his fortune?" she retorted more sharply than she had intended. But she was made nervous by how easily he was getting under her skin. If he stayed too much longer she didn't think she could withstand his powerful aura. The very last thing she wanted was for a man to turn her whole world inside out. Contact was too dangerous. He would never give her what she needed. He would eventually marry some beautiful young woman within his own circle. She knew there would be a long list for him to choose from.

He sensed her concealed agitation. "Is that what you *really* want, Sonya?" The force of his gaze pinned her in place.

"What I want is perhaps something I will never get," she said enigmatically. "Now would you excuse me for a moment? I want to get out of this tracksuit." From the moment she had met him, every instinct had warned her not to allow him to come close. She knew she couldn't deal with emotions that could not be contained.

"Take your time," he called after her as she started to move down the narrow passageway. "I'm going to take a look at your books." He crossed to the large timber book-case that stood against the end wall. It was jammed with books. "German, French, Russian, Hungarian, how weird is that?" he called after her. "No need to be in a rush to tell me."

"See how much you can work out on your own," she threw ironically over her shoulder.

When she returned she was wearing a long turquoise and lime-green dress that hung from shoestring straps over her bare shoulders. The bodice clung lovingly to her breasts, then fell in a fluid drop to her ankles. She wore little silver ballet shoes on her feet. Obviously she had run a brush through her hair, but the great thing was she had left it loose. "What languages do you speak?" he asked quietly, not taking his eyes from her. She looked so beautiful, so strangely *innocent*, he had to suck in his breath.

"A few." She moved quickly into the kitchen. There would now be a high barrier between them.

"You read Goethe and Schiller in the original? I saw that wonderful monument to them both when I was last in Germany. Then you have the French collection. A well-thumbed Flaubert's *Madame Bovary*, Victor Hugo, Dumas,

Gautier among others. A lot of Hungarian literature, Janos Arany, Kazinczy, Molnar, a very old chronical of Magyar affairs."

"You know perfectly well I have Hungarian blood."

"I know nothing of the sort," he lightly jeered. "Hungarian accent according to Rowena. Norwegian surname. Norwegian ancestry? What's the big secret anyway? What is it you're frightened of giving up? There has to be a better way, Sonya. Your manner, the extreme reserve, only adds fuel to the fire. It's as if you didn't exist up until five years ago."

"Maybe I'm on the run from villains," she suggested, preparing the coffee.

He shot her an impatient look. "I wouldn't be a bit surprised."

"Of course you wouldn't. You don't trust me one bit."

"How can I when you make yourself one-hundred-percent inaccessible? What sort of life have you had?"

He sounded as though it really mattered to him. That shook her. Her body was filling with shivery sensations.

"You must have had lovers?" How had they ever let her go?

She looked up very quickly from what she was doing, green eyes frosted. "Why make it sound as if I had a brigade of them? The truth is, I don't like men all that much."

"So you keep the ones you consider dangerous at a distance. It's the *why* I want to know. There's got to be an answer."

"Distance is effective," she said, pressing the button on the coffee machine.

"Generally speaking women who want distance don't give off high-octane sparks," he said dryly. "Not to men anyway. *You* do, Sonya. You know it. I know it."

She felt the heat that rushed into her cheeks. "How do you know I don't already hate *you*?"

"Okay, tell me," he invited. "*Do* you?"

She kept her eyes down. "Black or with cream?"

"All right, don't answer me," he said as though it was just what he expected. "Black, two sugars."

"Something with it?"

"No, thank you, Sonya. For God's sake come from behind that counter. There's not a lot of danger out here." How could he claim that, when the atmosphere was potentially explosive?

She gave him a cool look. "This *is* where I make the coffee."

"Looks more like you're barricading yourself in."

"I definitely am *not*."

"You definitely *are*," he contradicted.

"Well, we're enemies, aren't we? In a manner of speaking, of course."

He considered. "It might surprise you, Sonya, but I'm not gunning for you."

"What else would you call it?" She came around the counter, carrying the tray set with coffee things.

He stood up to take it from her, the brief touch of his hands on hers enough to soak her in warmth.

"On the coffee table, please," she said, trying to regain her habitual cool. "I hope it's the way you like it."

"What I'd like is for you to sit and talk to me," he said very seriously.

"I fancy our talk would turn into an interrogation." She shrugged. "You know my name, age, occupation, my address. What else do you need?"

"I have to say—*plenty.*" His tone hardened somewhat. "You're getting yourself into something here, Sonya, as

I've already warned you. You should be prepared. You told Marcus you'd ring him this evening."

"I will. No need to make it sound like a duty." She sat down on the opposite sofa, leaving her coffee on the table.

"Do you fully understand how much he cares for you?" he asked.

"Well, I care for him," she replied with a touch of aggression. "His humour, his gentle nature, his generosity, the brilliance of his mind. There aren't many men as gentle and courtly as Marcus. I feel safe with him."

"Will you marry him if he asks you?" He put it to her bluntly.

Her emerald eyes flashed fire. "Are you really entitled to an answer?"

"Please don't be cute."

"Cute? *Cute*? You must be crazy!" Tempestuously she leapt to her feet, her hair flying. "I am not like that. Why don't you answer *my* questions."

"I might if you sit down again." He was having difficulty keeping his own emotional balance. He felt desire coiled deep within him like a tempting serpent. It was imperative he keep his distance, adjust his moral compass in the right direction.

"So don't make me angry." Sonya sank down again, reaching for a silk cushion as if she might throw it at any moment. "My question: are you serious about your Paula or are you just stringing her along?"

That rankled. "Paula and I go back a long way."

"No doubt to the cradle." She gave a tiny mocking yawn. "Only it's you who should be paying attention. You're not behind the door handing out unsolicited advice, so I tell you as a favour, she's madly in love with you."

He gave her a long, intense look. "Does this mean I'm

under some sort of obligation to return her love? I've never told her I was. I am *not* stringing her along as you're suggesting. In my experience one only has to press a woman's hand for her to start hearing wedding bells. I've dated a lot of attractive women. Not so many of late, I'm afraid. I'm too damned busy."

"Why wouldn't you be, as your father's heir?" she commented. "Why does Paula Rowlands want to hurt me? Why would she say such words? I very much resent I'm 'after' you. One would think it was a hunt."

"In a way it is." He gave a brief laugh. "We're all out there looking, searching, hunting for a soul mate."

"And you've rejected everyone so far?"

He levelled an intense stare at her. "Haven't you?"

She looked down, a glow in her cheeks. "I admit I have kept to myself as much as possible."

"A woman as tantalizing as you, Sonya, would pretty much have to keep up her guard. Is that the attraction with Marcus? You feel with Marcus you can control the relationship? Is that how you feel?"

She gave a sad little smile. "I've never been able to control anything in my life." Some of the old bitterness and frustration began to surface. She regretted it, but family ghosts were slipping by her. "Drink your coffee," she urged. "It's going cold." She picked up her own cup, trying to shake off her nerves. The best way to protect herself was to stay perfectly cool. Even detached. "When do your parents return?" she asked politely.

"They're enjoying themselves so much they'll probably take another month. We have many good friends in the US."

"Have you told them about me?" Her tone was now so cool it almost snapped.

He shook his dark head. "But someone is bound to have

let them know, Sonya. My parents know everybody. Most of them were at the gala. Women love to pass on gossip. You made quite an impact. But you would have known that. In fact you invited it. Which is a bit of a paradox, given your extreme reserve. Then if that weren't enough you were wearing Lucy's emeralds."

"As lovely as they are, they are not the most beautiful emeralds in the world," she said with one of her elegant shoulder shrugs.

More role playing! He wondered. At times when her composure threatened to fail her, her slight accent became more pronounced.

"You've worn better?" he asked, his expression frankly sardonic.

She had the foolish impulse to run down to her bedroom and take the Madonna from its hiding place. She would show it to him: diamonds, rubies, emeralds, pearls, extravagantly beautiful, extravagantly precious. The Wainwrights, for all their wealth, had nothing like that.

"Hard for you to believe but maybe I have seen better."

"In the display windows of leading European jewellers, no doubt. The problem is, Sonya, they belonged to Lucy. My mother loved Lucy. They were great friends. It was an extraordinary thing for Marcus to offer them to you to wear."

"I'd never contemplated he would do such a thing." She was driven to defend herself. "He made it almost impossible for me to refuse. He was intent on my wearing them. More to the point, he would have known what effect that would have on all of you."

His chiselled mouth tightened. "It's time they never looked better," he added ironically.

"I wish now I'd offered a strong refusal. So I must expect your parents will be predisposed to dislike me?"

"I'm afraid so, Sonya." He couldn't deny it. "And dislike is the least of it. We're all very protective of Marcus. My father, *extremely* so."

"So, it's a catastrophe if Marcus falls in love with me?" She issued the challenge.

"The perceived catastrophe would be *you* don't love him," he retorted. "He's thirty years your senior. We've been over this, Sonya."

"I very much dislike the way you treat me." Her green eyes turned stormy. "Is a big age difference all that important? Surely what is important is that Marcus finds happiness. All this emphasis on sex—a sex life surely isn't the be-all and end-all of a marriage?"

"Of course it isn't, but it's a great help to be hungry for each other." His vibrant voice deepened. "You don't get it, do you? A lot of people are going to hate you, Sonya."

"Well, I think you and they are very very stupid!" She spoke with sudden fire, rising to her feet again, her willowy back ramrod straight.

From where did this woman get her class, her style, her apparently natural air of superiority? Her previous life couldn't have been one of tranquillity. She was forever on her guard. "I wish you to go." She gave an imperious flourish of her hand towards the door.

"Certainly." He rose to his splendid height, torn between anger and amusement. "You can show me out."

"I *will*!" There was an extraordinary intensity in her green eyes. Her head was spinning. Her body was alive with excitements, hungers. She moved swiftly ahead of him, so swiftly the tiny bow on one of her silver ballet shoes hooked on the fringe of the rug. She pitched forward, cursing her haste, only he caught her up from behind.

His strong arms encircled her for the second time that day. *Surrounded* her like a force field. Her heart leapt into her throat as he pulled her back against him, both of them facing the door.

"Tell me again you hate me," he murmured in a dark velvety voice.

The polished skin of his cheek rasped thrillingly against hers. Every ounce of strength, physical and mental, seemed to be draining out of her body. "You *are* hateful!" He was reading her reactions, she knew it. He was taking her to a place she had never gone before. Man, the traditional manipulator of women!

"Don't lie to me," he whispered against her ear.

The very air was spitting, crackling, with tension. "Don't you realize what you're doing?" Her mind was crashing. Her heart was crashing. For these brief moments she was beset by intolerable yearnings, abruptly made aware of the passionate red blood in her.

"David?" She tried to wrest away from him, but he held firm.

A certain contempt he felt for himself was no match for his desire for her. The heady incense of sex was an inciting vapour that hung in the air. There had to be countless instances of overwhelming temptation but he had never felt anything remotely like this before. There were only two possible options available to him. Let her go. Or give into this furious passion. She was bent forward over his arm. His arms had effectively locked her in. The tips of his fingers were pressing into the undersides of her beautiful high breasts. Still he didn't release her. It was almost as though he were under a spell with all his senses inflamed.

Sonya was frantic to settle on a course of action. Her knees were buckling under the onslaught. Heat had turned to *scorch*. The delta between her legs had turned moist. "David, you mustn't do this."

True. True. True.

The two of them were locked into an impossible attraction. He could feel her trembling. "I know," he said harshly, turning her to face him. It was a mistake. He had her exactly where he wanted her, only he knew he had to let her go. The pity was he couldn't find the time or space to regain control. With a half-maddened exclamation, he brought his dark head down low over hers, furious with himself that he wanted her so *badly*. The voice of reason had quietened into nothingness…

His kiss was fierce. He had her beautiful body in his arms, their two bodies, male and female, connecting in an extravagantly erotic way. His strong male drive was urging him on, fuelling him with energy. At some point he realized she was having difficulty coping with such an onslaught. He lifted his mouth fractionally from hers, allowing her to take breath…only he was back to kissing her. He had never kissed a woman so passionately. He hadn't even known he *could* reach such a level of wanting, needing. He was desperate for her response. His fingers twined in a handful of her hair, holding her face up to him. Her mouth was so sweetly, so silkily *lush* he couldn't drag his own away.

Stop. You've got to stop. Or be damned.

The voice in his head had increased to a warning blast.

This is the woman Marcus has come to love.

Madness to continue to hold her, but he was losing the battling against this wild rage of emotion. He wanted to sweep her up and carry her down the corridor to her bedroom. He wanted to strip her dress from her, ablaze with the desire to feel skin on skin. He wanted to kiss and caress her all over her naked body with its satiny white skin. For minutes there it had felt so completely *right*.

But it was hopelessly *wrong*. The verdict cold and hard.

How could he see people hurt? The future of the three of them was in jeopardy. The eternal triangle. Marcus, himself and Sonya, the woman they both wanted. Yet hadn't it been inevitable from the first moment their eyes met?

With a monumental effort he forced himself to let her go, aware he was breathing as heavily as if he had run the four-minute mile. Her beautiful hair was in total disarray, fanning out like a halo around her emotion charged face. She looked so vulnerable, so young, his heart smote him.

"Sonya, forgive me. I hadn't meant that to happen." They were like a pair of conspiratorial lovers filled with as much agony as ecstasy.

Her voice shook so badly, it betrayed her. Could it be possible he had deliberately engineered this, seeking her reaction? "You rich people are so ruthless!" Her distressed mind turned to *tactics*. "Who are *you* to drag me into your arms? What is your agenda? We both know you have one." She had lost sight of her own.

"Agenda? Don't talk rubbish." His response was curt. "You know damned well I'm attracted to you." He could have laughed at the sheer inadequacy of the word. Magnetized? Mesmerized? Spellbound?

"Now this is very interesting." She was transformed into a state of the utmost hostility. "*You're* attracted to *me*!" The entrenched defence mechanisms were back in place.

"Neither of us sought it," he said. "Neither of us wanted it. It just happened."

"Just happened?" she cried. "Oh, you're very convincing."

"So were *you*, just then, beautiful Sonya. Okay, I admit

my mistake. I was the aggressor. But it's too late now to make a fuss. I'm sorry if I hurt you." His dark eyes moved slowly over her body.

She took a deep shaky breath, feeling weak and ashamed. "You are mad, mad, *mad*!"

"You're so damned right," he agreed tonelessly, his handsome face taut.

"You are leaving."

It was a statement, not a question.

Still he turned back. "You'd prefer me to stay?" There was hard mockery in his brilliant eyes when the temptation to stay was overwhelming.

"You are *leaving*," she repeated. 'This is not your finest hour, David Wainwright."

"I agree. I'm afraid I overestimated my powers of self-control. So how do I go about making reparation? I'm too much of a gentleman to ask you to account for *your* behaviour. There's a lot of passion dammed up behind the Ice Princess façade, isn't there, Sonya? Floods of it!"

She felt as if she were thrashing about in a cage. "I've had enough! I know what you're up to. You are *not* exonerated. You are wanting me to fall in love with you. That is your strategy. I should have been prepared. After all, men have been preying on the weakness of women since the dawn of time. Your precious Marcus would be safe from my greedy clutches. How could dear sweet Marcus compare to you? I can't deny your sexual power. But I can refuse to succumb to it. I've had no ordinary life. I've had years and years of—" She had to break off, sick with herself, sick with him. She took a strangled intake of breath. "Don't ever touch me again!"

"But we can't forget the here and *now*." Some demon was in him. The way she spoke to him. The combative glitter in her emerald eyes. Who did she think she was? She affected him so powerfully in all the right ways. And all the wrong ways. Anger engulfed him. He pulled her back into his arms, outrage overcoming his natural protective feelings towards women. *His* sexual power? he thought grimly. What about *hers*?

His kiss was like a brand. Sonya tried to grit her teeth, but his tongue forced entry into her mouth. An avalanche of dark pleasure had her near collapsing against him.

Equally furiously he drew back. "I'd say you returned my kisses, you little fraud."

Without a second's hesitation she lifted her arm, hell-bent on leaving the imprint of her fingers on his handsome, hateful face.

He caught her wrist mid-flight. "Don't mess with me, Sonya," he rasped.

"And blessings on you too!" she cried. "Maybe I will marry your Marcus. Outrage your entire family, Lady Palmerston who has been so kind to me, your friends, your whole circle, that witch of a Paula Rowlands. Go grab her if you want to grab a woman. She's desperate for you to do it. But you can't have *me*."

He shot out a hand to grasp the door knob. "You sure about that?" he asked with a lick of contempt. "Are you *sure* you can cross me?"

She laughed, throwing up her chin. "Trust me, David Wainwright. I've had plenty of experience of villains."

It was an admission that sobered him entirely. "I suggest if one shows up, Sonya, you give me a ring." He couldn't have been more serious.

"What use are you to me?" The stormy expression in her green eyes became uncertain.

He opened the door. "If you're in trouble—any kind of trouble—you had better contact me," he said. "Whatever else I am, Sonya, I'm no villain."

CHAPTER FIVE

SONYA had never thought to see Paula Rowlands come into her shop, given Paula's vehement promise that would never happen, but lo and behold there she was!

Another catastrophic day?

And the timing was terrible! She was having lunch with Camilla in just over a half-hour. Paula wasn't alone. An older woman was with her, both of them stern faced, dressed to the nines. This was the mother from hell obviously. Family resemblance was apparent; the expressions were identical. They might have been called as witnesses in an unsavoury court case involving her.

Sonya acknowledged them with a calm nod, although her stomach muscles were tensing. She finished off wrapping a large bunch of stunning yellow heliconias. She had added some ginger foliage that had very interesting yellow strips for effect. She passed them across to her valued customer with a smile. "There you are, Mrs Thomas. You might use a few dark philodendron leaves if you have them at home," she suggested. "See how it goes."

Maureen Thomas nodded, very happy with the unusual selection. "These are splendid, thank you so much."

"My pleasure."

Mrs Thomas glanced in pleasant fashion at the two very

uppity looking women as she walked to the door. She might have been invisible. It amused her.

Marilyn Rowlands swooped to the counter, a mother protecting her young. "Look here, young lady," she said without preamble, "it's wrong what you're doing. You're only creating serious problems for yourself."

"Do I know you?" Sonya's brows arched.

Breathe deeply. Keep calm.

Marilyn's face clouded. "You *know* me. I'm Paula's mother." She might have been as easily recognisable as the Queen of England.

"Paula can't speak for herself, then?" Sonya asked politely.

"No cheek, young lady," Marilyn Rowlands said, thinking this girl was a whole lot more than she had been led to expect. She was amazingly beautiful, with an ultra-refined look. "I take insolence from no one," she warned, placing a heavily be-ringed hand on the counter.

A blue cloisonne bowl full of exquisite gardenias jumped. Sonya settled it.

What was it the Buddhists intoned to calm them?

Om...om...om.

"Do I have a need for concern here, Mrs Rowlands?" she asked. "There *is* a security guard who patrols these shops."

Marilyn's coiffed head shot back in outrage. "Are you threatening me?"

"I have a perfect right to refuse service to difficult people who come into my shop, Mrs Rowlands."

Paula belatedly entered the fray. "No one speaks to my mother like that. My father could have you out of here in no time."

"I doubt that," Sonya said.

"You leave my husband out of this," Marilyn Rowlands ordered, not averse to a slanging match.

Sonya was. "Mrs Rowlands, I'm asking you quietly to leave."

Marilyn Rowlands stood her ground. "First I need you to promise me you'll stop your little games."

"What games exactly?'

"You know very well. You're an opportunist."

"So what's in it for me?" Sonya asked.

Paula threw up her hands in triumph. "I *knew* it! Didn't I tell you, Mummy?" she cried as though her low opinion of Sonya had been vindicated.

Marilyn opened her Chanel handbag, and then pulled out a cheque book. "Don't attempt to double cross me, young lady. How much?"

"What's the best you can offer?" Sonya asked.

"Why, you're no better than a con woman," Marilyn Rowlands said with an overlay of contempt.

"Five hundred thousand dollars!" Sonya named a ridiculous figure. Who cared?

Marilyn frowned ferociously. "That's a bit steep."

"David, or Marcus?" Sonya asked, covering up her sick feeling.

"Both. Holt adores Paula."

"So I can't have Marcus?"

Marilyn Rowlands frowned as if a massive migraine was coming on. "How long have you been on the make? I repeat, you can have *neither*. They're way out of your league."

"And I know for certain Holt is going to marry me," Paula threw in for good measure.

Her mother focused on Sonya with eyes as cold and round as marbles. "Two hundred and fifty thousand dollars, my last offer. It would be a fortune to someone like you.

Quit the flower shop. Get yourself an education. Move on. Take the money. Shut up shop. Head for sunny Queensland. Lots of lotus eaters up there. We want you gone." She looked in her bag, found her Mont Blanc pen. "A lot of people want you gone. Especially the Wainwright clan."

"Listen to me a moment, Mrs Rowlands." Sonya spoke very quietly, but with a note in her voice that stopped Marilyn Rowlands in her tracks. "I've been leading you on. I'm not interested in you or your money. I find this whole episode extremely distasteful. What I want you to do now is walk quietly out of my shop. And never return."

"Excuse me!" Marilyn Rowlands gave vent to a growl she could well have learned from her Chihuahua.

"You have my word I won't mention this visit or the offensive things you've said."

Paula broke in again. Seething with jealousy. "Why don't you go back to where you came from? Some dingy European dump, I expect."

"Perhaps I should call the security man."

Marilyn Rowlands put up her hand. "That's enough, Paula," she said sternly. "Wherever this young woman came from, it was no dump." She looked back to Sonya. "Turn my proposal over in your head, Ms Erickson. You're no fool. You could see the sense of it some time soon. Holt's parents are due home soon. I'm a pussy cat compared to Holt's mother. As for his father! You poor girl, it would be a horrendous thing to cross him. I highly recommend you don't do it. Holt is everything in the world to them. *You* have no chance in the world of gaining admittance to *that* family, believe me."

Sonya gave Marilyn Rowlands a straight look. "The question is do I *want* to gain admittance, Mrs Rowlands. I haven't as yet decided the answer."

* * *

At the weekend Marcus suggested she come out on his boat. Local weather was holding gloriously calm and fine. "It hasn't been out for ages," he told her. "You *must* come."

The "boat" turned out to be a svelte and racy 128 yacht designed years before by a famous ex-patriot who went on to become a world legend. Marcus, looking a good ten years younger in his tailored jeans and blue sports shirt beneath a gold buttoned navy blazer, showed her around the *Lucille Anne* with careless pride. "I used to be a good sailor in my day. Let it go. I'm sorry about that now. David is a brilliant sailor. He should take you out some time. You don't get seasick?'

"I'm sure one couldn't get seasick on this magnificent yacht." She smiled.

The *Lucille Anne* had three decks of cabins and saloons. The main saloon, marvellously comfortable, was panelled in walnut with touches of macassar ebony. Apart from the plush master suite there were four guest staterooms. On the teak laid aft deck reached by a gleaming stainless steel stairway with a balustrade, there was casual furniture and a swimming platform Sonya wasn't about to use any time soon.

"Lucy and I used to take it to the Mediterranean when young David was on holidays," Marcus told her with a smile of remembrance. "We looked on him as our own child. He was a remarkable boy. A remarkable young man."

"You love him?"

"Oh, yes!" Marcus confirmed quietly. "David is every inch the man we all wanted him to be."

It turned out to be a relaxing day spent in total luxury. A superb seafood lunch was served on the glass-topped oak table accented in ebony in the dining saloon. Afterwards they adjoined to the aft deck with its comfortable arrangements of chairs and wide teak table that held a low black bowl filled with pink and yellow hibiscus.

"You look happy." Marcus spoke in such a deep tender voice it was a clear giveaway. Sonya was wearing navy jeans with a navy and white T-shirt, white sneakers on her feet. A casual outfit on a beautiful young woman with a willowy body. She could have earned a fortune modelling clothes. Apparently that held little allure for her. She was seemingly content in her world of flowers.

Sonya turned her head lazily. "I am. You're lovely company, Marcus. Thank you so much for asking me."

"I want to do everything you want, Sonya," he announced, in a fervent voice. "And I want to do it *now*. I know you don't love me. I couldn't ask for that, but you are fond of me?"

Sonya sat straight, her heart thudding. This was an opportunity most women would give their eye teeth for. Only she wasn't at all sure she was one of them. It wasn't an everyday event to be proposed to by a millionaire. Some would be ecstatic. Only she had developed a taste of passion, shameful though the memory was. Affection was at the heart of her very real feelings for Marcus. Never passion.

Shove all thoughts of David Wainwright from your mind. Do it now, her inner voice instructed.

Marilyn Rowlands had made a point of telling her she would never fit into David Wainwright's world. In all probability she had spoken the truth. His parents would have their own ideas about their adored son's future.

"No, let me finish," Marcus said, sensing her perturbation. "I'm a rich man. But with no woman in my life to love, I might as well be dirt poor. I fell in love with you the instant I walked into your shop."

"Marcus!" She held out her hands like a supplicant,

palms up. How could she hurt this gentle man? He wanted her. More importantly he could protect her if ever the time came. She knew Laszlo wouldn't rest until he had tracked her down; made certain she wasn't in possession of the Andrassy Madonna. She had lived with the fear he would eventually find her. He could already be closing in.

"Please listen," Marcus begged. "You don't talk about yourself. In my experience people who have suffered deep traumas never talk. Maybe they can't. I know you have a story, but I'm content to wait until you're ready to tell me about it. I don't care what it is. I don't care what you've done—if indeed you've done anything. I want to marry you, Sonya. I want to look after you. There is still time for me to father a child. You will want for nothing."

Except passionate love.

Is that so bad? Don't you read the headlines, girl? Celebrities passionately in love one moment suddenly spitting venom and selling their stories to the magazines. They move on to someone else to fuel their tank. I ask you, what is love? Where does the love go?

"You don't have to answer me now. I can see I've stunned you. You can have all the time you want."

She had to control a desire to weep. "Marcus, you've *honoured* me." At the same time she couldn't help thinking maybe what he really wanted was a daughter. This man was terribly lonely.

Marcus must have guessed her thoughts. "Sonya, I love you as a *woman*," he said. "A beautiful, gifted woman, and most hopefully the mother of our child. You needn't fear I couldn't give you a child. My poor little Lucy couldn't get pregnant. She was never strong. Lucy would want me to be happy. She was the sweetest human being."

All sorts of emotions tugged at her. She had to remember what her life had been. Marcus could change all that. She spoke earnestly. "Marcus, your family might very well see me as an opportunist. You're a rich man. You're years older than I am. They would question that."

"Let them!" he said scornfully. "As long as *you* don't question it. I don't give a damn what anyone thinks. I'm in love with you. I don't even care David has his concerns. That's how much I want you."

So David, traitor, has spoken of his concerns!

"No Wainwright has power over me, Sonya," Marcus said firmly. "You, however, *do.*"

Say something. Say something. Silence will give him hope.

He reached for her hand. "If you marry me I'll do everything in my power to keep you safe and happy. That, I swear."

It was an enormously touching moment. Would it be so terrible to marry Marcus?

Give yourself time to think. Marcus Wainwright is a good man. How many of them are about?

Days passed. She was kept very busy in the shop. She had an assistant, a single mother with two children, aged seven and nine, who did part-time work that fitted in with her mothering schedule. Penny had received some training in a suburban flower shop. She was very good with the customers, efficient at what she did and if she lacked a certain imagination it didn't matter all that much to Sonya, who could always do a bit of tweaking. As a single mother Penny needed the work. Sonya had been happy to give it to her.

Midweek Marcus took her out to dinner in one of those restaurants where the price list would give the average person a heart attack. And that didn't include the hefty tip. Marcus looked very handsome in his professorial fashion, his face radiating his pleasure and pride in her company.

His high spirits would have been apparent to all who gave him a little friendly wave as they passed, or those who bent closer over the table to make a comment, most probably acid.

The longer this goes on, the harder it gets. For you and him. You owe him an answer. You have to make up your mind what it's going to be.

The whole situation, so jubilant to Marcus, was weighing heavily on her mind.

The entrée, a selection of *teeny* morsels, delicious enough, but served in what was nearly a platter. It seemed to her ridiculously pretentious. She reached for her wine glass, noticing at that moment the maître d' showing a tall, stunningly handsome man and his extremely pretty companion to a table. Her decision was made for her.

It has to be a no. Of course it has to be a no. Married to a man you do not love with the prospect of seeing the man you're so powerfully drawn to on every family occasion. Sheer madness!

"Good Lord, it's David!" Marcus was saying delightedly as he stood up to attract his nephew's attention. "David!" he called. "He has Emma Courtney with him, Sonya. Lovely girl, Emma. She's nuts about him, as the saying goes. I should know. I'm nuts about you." He laughed, colour in his lean cheeks. "I'll introduce you."

It was the very last thing Sonya wanted. She sat back, desperate to achieve some semblance of calm.

David Wainwright will marry a young woman much like the one he's out with tonight.

Get that through your head.

His hand at Emma's elbow, Holt led the way to his uncle's table. The shock of seeing her again was as painful, as piercing as an arrow shot straight to the heart.

You fool!

His warning voice kicked in, determined on giving him hell. She was wearing the standard little black dress but her radiant beauty and her colouring made the dress look as if it were worth every last cent of a million dollars. Marcus was beaming with pride. It was obvious he would do anything for her. Lay down his life if need be. Not only was she far and away the most beautiful woman in the room, she was highly intelligent. If she was after position and security, a half-share of Marcus's money, it was as good as in her hand. From a florist shop to chatelaine of one of the most beautiful houses in a city full of beautiful houses. Money beyond her wildest dreams would be at her disposal. For all he knew the wedding date had already been set.

He had to bring all his concentration to bear just on saying hello.

Marcus gripped his shoulder. "What a surprise to see you, David. How are you, Emma? You look lovely as usual." Marcus moved a pace to kiss Emma's cheek. She was a true redhead with lovely bright blue eyes.

"Sonya." Holt acknowledged her with a slight bow. She gave him a cool smile.

Still playing the aristocrat for all she was worth. It was a sterling performance. He had to give her that. "I'd like you to meet a friend of mine, Emma Courtney. Emma, Sonya Erickson." He made the introduction.

Emma rated a real smile. It lit up Sonya's beautiful face like the sun sparkling off ice. "Nice to meet you, Emma."

"You too, Sonya. I've heard a lot about you." Emma was looking at Sonya with open admiration.

"I take it David is the one giving the information?" Sonya kept the smile on her face.

"All *good* things." Emma gave a tiny triangular smile. It

could have meant she'd had a few words with others, like
Paula Rowlands, whom she no doubt knew.

A pleasantry or two more and they moved off. Emma
glanced back and gave a little friendly wave.

"Lovely girl!" Marcus enthused, sitting down again.
"I'm so glad David isn't serious about Paula. You have to
be careful with those Rowlands women. Though I have to
say Paula can be extremely nice when the mood takes her.
Emma had better look out. Paula has always been wildly
jealous of anyone who even looked sideways at David."

Tell me about it.

"Then she has a battle on her hands. Every woman in
the room looked up the moment he walked in."

"You too?" Marcus shot her a quick intent look.

"Why not? I was enjoying it," she lied. "I had my own
entry tracked."

"You'll have to get used to it, dearest girl." He relaxed.
"It might be a nice idea to meet up with them after dinner.
Go on somewhere. What do you think?"

No way could she handle that. "No nightclubs, Marcus,"
she said, pretending a modicum of regret. "I should be
a good girl and go home. Early start at the markets tomorrow."

"Of course, my dear." His hand covered hers across the
table. "Though I hope you'll find the time to pop into the
house with me for ten minutes. I have something to show
you. Jensen will drive you home, of course."

"Ten minutes, Marcus. No more."

"Splendid!" He raised his glass to her.

Whatever Marcus had in mind she thought she could
deal with it.

Her arrangements, she noticed with satisfaction, were still
amazingly fresh. There was such a glow about Marcus.

Unusual colour in his cheeks. For a very dignified, contained man, it was only too clear he was excited. Indeed he had come alive with exhilaration. He was a great collector. Perhaps he had acquired a new painting. Possibly for her? He knew she was passionate about good art.

"Sit down, my dear," he invited, pulling out an armchair covered in blue silk damask. "I had the most wonderful dream the other night. I dreamt you said yes to my proposal of marriage. Next day I went out and bought this." Slowly he withdrew from his inner breast pocket a small jewellery box. "Wasn't it Freud who said we should place great faith in our powerful dreams?" he asked, not waiting for her answer. "Sonya, dearest girl, I want you to wear this as a token of my everlasting love. Give me your hand, my dear. I'm sure it will be a perfect fit."

Was there any tactful way of offering a rebuff? *No*, was the short answer. Only for the life of her she couldn't seem to utter a word. Her mouth and throat had gone so dry she wanted to leap up to go and find a glass of water.

"There!" Marcus said with great satisfaction. "What did I tell you? Perfect. Don't you think so?"

Sonya was astounded. The diamonds were like chunks of Arctic ice. She stood up, feeling as though her heart had left her chest. "Marcus, is this what I think it is?"

"My dearest girl, you *know* it's an engagement ring," he said with loving indulgence. "I'm very serious about wanting to marry you. If I hesitate some other lucky man will sweep you up. I can't have that. You are my great chance at happiness."

Suddenly she wasn't at all sure he could withstand the shock of an abrupt refusal. He was so *happy*, even if he had rather jumped the gun. But then he would have lived a life when he could have just about anything he ever wanted.

"Were diamonds a mistake?" he asked, seeing her

confusion. "You will have the emeralds, my dear," he assured her. "But I thought *diamond* for the ring. They're the finest money can buy."

Distress flashed into her green eyes. "No, diamonds aren't the mistake, Marcus," she said slowly, reasoning she had best get this over with. "It's—" She broke off in horror as Marcus bent over, clutching his chest. "Marcus, what is it?" She flew up from her chair, to put her arms around him. She held him tight. "You're in pain."

"Nothing, nothing." Marcus tried to shrug off whatever ailed him. Only the high colour in his cheeks had turned to grey.

Sonya made her decision. "I'm going to call the ambulance. We need to get you to a hospital."

Marcus wasn't having that. "No, no, Sonya. I forbid it," he gasped. "A bit of chest pain. Not severe. Most probably heartburn. I don't normally eat dessert. It was too rich."

She wasn't convinced. "It's important you be checked out as soon as possible," she insisted, truly panicked and afraid for him. "Every moment counts. Let me call the ambulance."

"No," he said emphatically. "I'm feeling better already. I have a touch of anaemia, you know. Not enough iron."

"What about your doctor?" she persisted, not liking this one bit. "I could ring him. It's not late. I can't leave it like this, Marcus. Are you on any medication? I'll get you a glass of water."

By sheer will power Marcus pulled himself together. He sank back on the sofa. "You could try David. It's only discomfort, dear. Don't please panic. It's not a suspected heart attack, if that's what's worrying you. I know the symptoms. It's all the excitement, I suppose."

Please, God, let that be so!

Sonya ran to the kitchen, where she poured a glass of

water. "What's David's number?" she asked when she returned. Swiftly she unknotted Marcus's tie, then the top button of his shirt. Next she put the glass into his hand. "Medication?"

"I'm fine, Sonya," he insisted. "Please don't fuss, my dear." Marcus blew out his cheeks.

"I'll get David." Sonya ran to the landline in the kitchen and rang the number. Fear was pouring into her. She didn't like the look of Marcus, no matter what he said. She should be ringing the ambulance whether he forbade it or not. David would most probably still be with Emma.

He answered on the fourth ring. "It's Sonya," she said, not trying to control her anxiety. "I'm at the house with Marcus. He's taken a sick turn. He won't let me ring the ambulance. He forbids it. He wants you. I'm going to ring his doctor."

"Leave that to me," he said in a clipped voice. "I'll be there in under ten minutes. I'm not far away."

When Sonya returned to the drawing room Marcus was still on the sofa, his torso slumped back, his right leg extended.

"Sit up straight, Marcus," Sonya advised, going to him. "David is coming. He's going to ring your doctor. They'll be here shortly." She held his hand within her own. "I love you, Marcus," she found herself saying. "You're a lovely man."

They were still sitting, holding hands, when David strode in, followed by the doctor. David stood over them, his expression grave. The doctor went straight to his patient. He made a quick check. "I'm getting you to hospital, old man. Just to be sure."

"I don't want to go, Bart," Marcus insisted. "I want to sit here with Sonya for ever."

"Trust me, Marcus," the doctor said. "You're better off

in hospital. David has already called the ambulance. If I'm not mistaken it's turning into the drive."

"We'll follow in my car," David said, watching Sonya gently withdraw her hand from his uncle's. On the fourth finger of her left hand was a magnificent diamond engagement ring, a spectacular central stone flanked by dazzling smaller stones.

Acute anxiety for his uncle was overlaid by a bitter torrent of anger. He could hardly bear to look at her. There was the proof. She'd snagged Marcus hook, line and sinker.

"What are you all thinking of?" Marcus was trying hard to smile. "I'll be as right as rain in another half-hour."

"You've not been looking after yourself as well as you should have, Marcus," Bart Abbott said. "You'll have to spend the night. I want to run a few tests."

CHAPTER SIX

THEY were only granted a few minutes alone with Marcus before he was whisked away. Sonya was greatly heartened by the fact he looked a little better and he was safely in hospital where he belonged.

David completely ignored her.

"I can get a cab," she said, when they were out in the night air.

"You'll get mugged wearing *that ring*," he said curtly. "Come with me." He took hold of her arm.

The contempt in his voice made her blood boil. "Take your hand off me, David," she ordered.

He brought them both to an abrupt halt. "Don't start here. Don't start *now*," he warned. "I'm taking you home. I have no choice. I never leave a woman on her own at night. Besides, Marcus would confidently expect it of me to see you home. I need to do everything in my power to keep his fiancée safe."

"*No* fiancée," she flashed back.

"I would think that damned great ring is a sure sign of an engagement," he challenged harshly. "Once we're in the car I can take another look. Perhaps it's the grandest friendship ring of all time."

"Maybe it was meant that way." She was angry enough to say anything.

He hit the remote, unlocking his car. "Get in."

It was useless to protest. He meant business. "Aren't you interested in hearing *my* side of the story?" she asked as she tried to buckle her seat belt, all fingers and thumbs with nerves.

With a muffled exclamation he did it for her, then he started the engine, turning a taut profile. "What the hell is wrong with you?" he asked with severity.

"I might ask you the same question," she retorted, refusing to give him the psychological advantage. "You're all churned up and it isn't *only* Marcus's sick turn, upsetting as it is. It's the *ring* that's bugging you. So does he have a heart condition or what?"

He didn't answer until they were out onto the road. "Not that I know of," he said tersely. "Bart is right. Marcus hasn't looked after himself in years. We all thought he was committing a form of slow suicide after Lucy died. I know he's had to have a course of B12 injections. Iron. Ah, what the hell? The sick turn is bound to have happened because he's worked himself into a lather over *you*."

"That's right, blame me. It's not unexpected like Marcus giving me the ring was. You need a scapegoat. He's only fifty-five, isn't he?" she challenged angrily. "He isn't seventy or eighty!"

He threw her a scathing glance. "I ask you. Would seventy or eighty have been too much mileage on the clock for you? What about ninety? Would you have said yes, then?"

She drew in a ragged breath. "I haven't said yes now. I really don't appreciate being insulted. Marcus asked me in for a few minutes. We went into the drawing room. I sat down. Next thing, Marcus reached into his pocket, and before I could manage a word he's shoving a ring on my finger."

He made a sound of utter disbelief. "That must have shocked you out of your mind, Sonya darling."

The *darling* was a dark insult, but her heart gave a crazy jolt. "This is no time for us to fight, surely? I'm very fond of Marcus. He's a good, kind man, but I didn't ask him to fall in love with me. It took me a while to even see it coming."

"But you did see eventually, Sonya," he jeered. "You knew you had him in the palm of your hand. Now you've got the pay-off."

She was so angry she felt like jumping out of the car. "Here, have it!" she cried tempestuously as she wrenched off the ring. "It weighs a ton. You have it. It'll be a lot safer with you." She put it into the glovebox.

His smile was one of outright mockery. "You're lost to the stage, Sonya. But tell me, is there any history of psychotic behaviour in your family? You have to have one, even if they're tucked well out of sight."

"Oh, I've got one all right," she answered through clenched teeth. "You wouldn't know about the sort of people I've had to live with, David Wainwright with your life of privilege, loved and admired on all sides. You wouldn't know much about the kind of relatives *I* have."

"Professional con artists, I suspect," he said when it was cruel. "A crime family, maybe? Some in prison?"

"Why don't you just *drive*?"

She had the door of the Mercedes open before he had come to a complete stop.

"That was stupid," he reprimanded her, getting out. "I'll see you to your door."

"You stay here." Her hostility was in plain sight. "I'm in shock."

"Me too. But while Marcus is out of commission, I'm

responsible for the safety of his fiancée," he said with suave contempt.

She threw up her shining head. "What part of 'I'm in shock' don't you understand?"

"Let's go up," he said, moving purposefully towards her.

Had she resisted, she wouldn't have been in the least surprised had he thrown her over his shoulder.

A couple from the first floor was waiting for the lift. Good evenings were exchanged. The young woman could scarcely drag her eyes off Holt. Her partner was so busy staring at Sonya when the lift stopped at their floor he forgot to get out. His girlfriend gave him a sharp reminder.

"I don't think I'll lose my way if I walk myself to my door," Sonya said with heavy sarcasm. The lift had stopped at her floor. The door opened.

He held the diamond ring in his hand. He was staring down at it. "I can't keep this. It was given to you."

"Okay, I have to give it back!" Sonya's voice was a blend of anguish and anger. "I'm not making excuses for myself, David, but really Marcus presumed a great deal."

"Oh, wake up!" he exhorted her. "You knew what you were getting into." He took hold of her arm, walking her down the quiet corridor. "Give me the key."

"I won't let you in if it's the last thing I do," she said with vehemence.

"What are you frightened of?" His reply held a taunt.

"What are *you* frightened of?" She stared up into his fathomless dark eyes.

"Ruining everything for everybody, maybe," he said bleakly.

It shocked her. She stood back as he opened the door.

He pulled her in, shutting them into the quiet of the apartment. The fragrance she was wearing was swirling about in the air between them. It might have had the power of a drug. "Then there's *this*!" He was caught up by an unstoppable surge. It had him pressing her slender body back against the closed door.

"Oh, yes, there's *this*!" Colour lit her flawless white skin. The tension between them was palpable, electric. Once again they were in a dangerous place, the shadowy turbulence growing greater.

"I'm waiting for you to stop me," he challenged. Adrenalin was flooding his veins. He manoeuvred his body ever closer to hers, the softness of a woman, the hard musculature of a man.

She turned her head from side to side, straining to keep some measure of control over the situation. "Even if I *screamed* it wouldn't stop you."

"Not that you're about to scream," he taunted, lifting his arms to position them on both sides of her blonde head. "You're pinned in, Sonya." She was staring up at him with her beautiful mesmeric eyes. "How long have I known you?" he asked, astonished by how little time had passed.

"Maybe you knew me in another life?" Her voice dropped low.

Another trick? Her voice was magic, the little foreign accent, the wide range of intonations, the pitch. That was the trouble with powerful attraction. The alarming way it took control.

"Strangely enough, I believe it." He cupped the globe of her small breast in his hand. Then with a muffled exclamation he bent his head and crushed her captive silken mouth….

Sparks lit into a conflagration. Sensation was boundless; a wild clamouring in the blood that beat up waves of heat. It was as if every single light, every appliance in the apartment were turned on and *burning*, sucking in all the air. She gave a little moan, thinking nothing could ever be the same again. Her breasts were throbbing under his urgent caressing hands, the nipples gone cherry-hard when she felt her flesh were actually dissolving…

If the ringing phone had not penetrated the thickly meshed web they were caught into, he didn't know what would have happened. One minute they were mindlessly devouring each other, the next they were forced to break apart, breathless and trembling, trying to make the adjustment to the real world.

"That's the phone," she said, now humiliated by her headlong response to him.

He laughed at the sheer ridiculousness of it. "Don't answer it."

"I should." She shook her head, trying to clear it. Her legs were so weak it was an effort to reach the kitchen. When she picked up the receiver, she heard a woman's familiar voice, speaking with urgency.

"Sonya, it's Rowena. Would David be with you? I've had a call from the hospital. Marcus has been admitted."

"Then you know he had a sick turn, Lady Palmerston," Sonya said. "He gave us such a fright. I'll put David on. He brought me home."

"Thank you, dear."

She held out the phone to David. He took it, catching her around the waist and locking her into his grip. She freed herself none the less, moving away to allow him to speak in private. For years she had known the desperation of flight. Of always being on the run from those who would do her harm. She had never known the desperation of passion. He had felt it as much as she.

It was quiet on the balcony. She had filled it with a

luxuriant array of plants in large pots; flowering baskets she had attached to the brick wall. She stood in the night air, tears gathering in her eyes. She had long regarded crying as an intolerable indulgence. It had never helped her. Now she found herself on the verge of tears. For years she had told herself she wasn't scared of anything. But she *was* scared. She was scared of the depth of feeling she had for David Wainwright. She knew nothing would come of the violent attraction they felt for each other. It could only end badly. She was very worried about Marcus as well. Worried about what she would have to tell him. But when? For ghastly moments earlier that night she'd thought Marcus was about to suffer a heart attack. As it was, they wouldn't know the results of his tests for days.

You're in over your head, girl.

She had to give Marcus his ring back. There was faint conciliation in the thought Marcus should not have taken her acceptance as a given. But then the rich were different from everyone else. She put up a hand to pull the pins from her coiled hair. That done, she pressed her hands to her face. Sometimes life was merciless. She didn't love Marcus. Not in any romantic way. She did love David. In every way possible. Only it was Marcus who had given her the ring. Marcus who wanted to marry her. David didn't. He wanted nothing from her. But *sex*.

She still had her eyes closed when David came behind her, pulling her hands from her face. "You're crying." He flicked a salty tear off her cheek with his finger, placing it on his tongue. The cloud of erotica surrounding them was dense.

"It isn't with happiness," she said, turning to confront him. "What are we doing, David? I can see no way out of this short of disappearing."

"Isn't that what you've done before?"

His glittering eyes and his tone made her nerves jangle. "God, I hate you," she muttered.

"Just like I hate you," he returned in an openly self-mocking voice. "Isn't it better to hate me than love me if you're going to marry Marcus?"

"That will be *my* decision." Let him believe what he wanted to believe. It was a certain protection. "What is love really?" she asked.

He laughed briefly. "I have to let that one go at the moment, Sonya. But I can tell you a hell of a lot about wanting a woman."

"Marcus *wants* me but his kind of love I can't return," she said, torn by pity and sadness.

"Then you have to tell him."

His voice cut like a lash. "You want I should do it in the morning?" she challenged with a return of spirit. "Then you could all breathe a great sigh of relief. You don't fool me, David. It's not the time to upset Marcus. You know that as well as I do."

The truth of it made him angry. Yet desire for her was becoming something ungovernable. How could he be so uncaring of his uncle? "I have to go, Sonya," he rasped. "In another minute I'll pick you up and take you to bed."

"What, and betray Marcus?"

She threw up her head in a way now familiar to him. "That's *why* I'm going," he bit off. "I'm not proof against your witchcraft."

"So go, then." A soft poignancy replaced the anger in her voice. "How will it end, David?"

Abruptly the wild clamour that was in him turned to an even odder tenderness. He found himself turning back to cup her face in his hands. "I can't think about it right now, Sonya. I truly can't. We have to find out what's going on with Marcus."

"He was so excited! It was a flag signalling trouble."

She was the very image of lamentation. It caused his anger to flash back. "Has Marcus ever *kissed* you? I mean, *really* kissed you?" There was conflict here. The disloyalty associated with having to ask; the fear of how he would handle it if the answer was above and beyond *yes*.

She threw up her head. He would *never* give his trust. "This love affair is in Marcus's head. His life has been so lonely, for a woman, I mean. I know you all love him. It's extraordinary when you think about it. A kiss on the cheek, dinner, a few outings, one day on his yacht, and suddenly he can't part with me."

Holt forced his hands to drop to his sides. "Look at you! Why would he?" he asked harshly. "That's what falling in love is all about, Sonya." He moved with purpose to the door. He had to get away from her *fast*. Hunger for her was at cyclone-force, a headwind that could drive him back to her.

"I am *not* going to marry Marcus," she called after him.

"You need to marry someone." His retort was delivered with quick fire. "It doesn't do for a woman like you not to be safely contained."

They learned early the next morning Marcus had suffered a heart attack. He would be released in a few days, allowing time for the battery of tests. A top cardiac specialist had been called in. Sonya took flowers and fruit to the hospital. When she arrived at his private room she could see Lady Palmerston was there, looking, as ever, marvellous and so stylish in her tailored suit, slim black skirt, black and white jacket.

Marcus's face lit up. Lady Palmerston's did not. "Marcus

has just been telling me you're engaged?" she said, looking towards Sonya.

It was a far cry from the warm friendly tone Sonya had become used to. "I think Marcus has to give me time to catch my breath, Lady Palmerston," she said, moving to the bed to kiss Marcus's cheek. "How are you feeling, Marcus?"

"Much better," he said, his eyes dazzled by her youth and beauty. "Sorry I gave you and David such a fright. It was just a warning, the specialist said. I'm going to do *exactly* as he says. Life is too sweet."

"I'm sure the first thing is to put all excitements out of your mind, Marcus," Rowena said with a touch of severity. "A bit of quiet is called for."

"Now, now, Aunty dear." Marcus waved an affectionate hand at her. "I've had enough quiet all these years. The flowers are splendid, Sonya." He turned his head to admire them. Sonya had assembled six or seven red torch ginger flowers with some beautiful big glossy pinkish-red anthurium flowers and a few exotic tropical leaves. She intended to place them near the window.

"I have a vase with me," she said, lightly touching Marcus's hand. If only, if only he *hadn't* fallen in love with her. She did so want him as a friend. "I'll just fill it with water."

Less than ten minutes later a nurse came to the door. "Time for a rest now, Mr Wainwright," she said, crisply pleasant, but her eyes whipped over Rowena and Sonya with the message, *Time to leave.*

The lift to the ground floor was crowded, visitors, staff, a doctor in a pin-striped suit looking as though he was very important in the scheme of things. Noise and bustle everywhere. A hospital was never truly silent. Peace was hard to find. They were outside the hospital, walking to one of the parking areas, before Lady Palmerston spoke.

"You might tell me what this is all about, Sonya. An engagement?" She lifted her arched brows, her expression grave, but withholding judgment.

"I'm sorry, Lady Palmerston. I didn't see it coming."

"Call me Rowena, dear," Rowena said impatiently. "Marcus of all people to totally lose his head," she lamented. "Why, you're hardly more than a child."

"I'm twenty-five."

"A great age!" Rowena scoffed. "Marcus is thirty years older."

"So what should I have done?" Sonya implored. "I thought I had found a friend. I wasn't looking for a partner."

"Good Lord, Sonya, you must have had some idea where it was all going? An intelligent young woman like you."

"I regret I didn't speak out earlier. Initially it was the last thing I expected. I admire Marcus. He's a dear, distinguished man. Not an easy thing to tell him what he didn't want to hear. In my own defence I have to say I didn't encourage him. I didn't give him to understand our friendship was moving to another stage. Surely a smile isn't a big come-on? Enjoyment in good conversation? Sharing the things we have in common? I know all about loss, just as Marcus does. The trouble with rich people is they think they can have anything and *anyone* they want." She waved an agitated hand in front of her face.

Rowena considered. "There may be a touch of that," she frankly admitted. "But why, oh, why did you wear Lucy's emeralds, Sonya? That was a *huge* mistake. You've no idea how much gossip that caused."

"Gossip won't kill me," she said hardily. "People can say what they want." Sonya lifted her head to give Rowena a high mettled look. "Marcus was insistent. I had no idea the necklace would be so grand. There was such a look of pleasure in his eyes. For a moment I thought he was even on the verge of tears. I should have refused, but I was loath to take that light out of his face. My mistake."

"Well, it certainly put you in the line of fire," Rowena said quietly. "All of a sudden people are intensely interested in you. Who *are* you exactly? They all know now you're a florist. In my view the best florist in town, but a working girl."

"So, tough to be a working girl!" Sonya exclaimed with a satirical edge. "Naturally I masterminded a plan to land myself a millionaire."

Rowena took Sonya's arm. "My dear, you know as well as I do, it's every other young woman's goal to marry a millionaire."

"It is not mine." Sonya enunciated the words very clearly. "As it happens no one, including you, Lady Palmerston, knows the extent of my finances."

"How *would* I know?" Rowena asked in exasperation. "You never talk about yourself, Sonya. It's as though you're afraid to let anyone come near. I can see your attraction to Marcus. Marcus wouldn't have pressed you for information. I'm here for you, my dear. I like you. More, I've come to care for you. I readily understand how you've come to find a place in Marcus's heart. But your life before you came to this country appears to be a closed book. You're obviously well bred—" She broke off as if bewildered by Sonya's stand.

"I promise you, Lady Palmerston, I will tell you all about myself when I can." Sonya gently pressed her arm.

"So, no Rowena?" Rowena smiled.

Sonya's expression was intense. "I have such respect for

you, Lady Palmerston, I think I should work up to calling you Rowena."

"As you wish, my dear." Rowena glimpsed another Sonya, a young woman from a different background, a different world. Sonya gave such an impression of poise, of near regal self-assurance, then, out of the blue, a hint of a scared little girl. What did it all mean?

Two days after Marcus Wainwright was discharged from hospital he suffered, as others in similar circumstances had suffered before him, the one fatal heart attack. Even with a warning his death came as a pulverizing shock.

David received the news first from Marcus's distraught housekeeper, who found him lying on his side in bed. No sign of life, beyond any doubt. The housekeeper had once been a nursing sister.

From then on he took charge. News of the death of Marcus Wainwright couldn't be contained. His parents had to be advised. He fully expected them to return on the first available flight. He didn't tell them when he rang Marcus had fallen in love with a beautiful young woman decades his junior. He didn't divulge the fact Marcus had given her a magnificent diamond engagement ring. That definitely would have to wait. The entire Wainwright clan had to be advised. A hell of a thing. This was a tragedy that had been waiting to happen. Too late Marcus had come to a decision to take good care of himself.

Then of course there was Sonya.

Sonya was in for a very bad time unless he could control the media.

He knew from long experience he couldn't. The media would have a field day. And what of Marcus's will? If Marcus had been so sure he could persuade Sonya to marry him, wouldn't he have had the family solicitors draw up a new will? Sonya would surely be a beneficiary. He knew in the existing will he had been the principal beneficiary. Marcus had told him. If Marcus had had a new will drawn up it could be argued in court—if it ever came to that—Marcus was a sick man, indeed a dying man, infatuated by a young woman decades his junior. Marcus had been in a state of high confusion. How could a strange young woman of no background lay claim to what could very well be a substantial part of a considerable fortune? The inferences drawn would inevitably be that Sonya had worked on Marcus to change his will.

His mouth went dry at the thought of what his parents would make of it all. Both were formidable people to be approached with nigh on reverence. Grief might very well turn to outrage. Sonya might be an extremely beautiful, highly intelligent young woman with an unmistakable look of good breeding, but he and Rowena between them knew very little about her. One would have thought she was an orphan without family. Once the news broke she would go from an unknown to a high-profile woman. The woman in Marcus Wainwright's life.

By the time the press finished with her there would be nowhere to hide.

He didn't want to tell her over the phone. That would be too cruel. Though he couldn't spare the time he took a taxi to the trendy shopping conclave where she had her florist shop. No time for him to find a park for his own car.

Sonya knew, the instant she caught sight of David, something was very wrong. Her heart began a relentless banging against her ribs. No one was in the shop. She had been busy earlier on, now she was grateful for the lull.

"It's Marcus, isn't it?" She searched his brilliant dark

eyes. He was noticeably pale beneath his deep tan. "He's had a relapse?"

"Worse than that, Sonya." He held her eyes, feeling a heavy sense of guilt along with the grief. He wanted her as he had never wanted anyone before. "There's no easy way to tell you this. Marcus is dead."

"No, no, dear God, no!" She staggered, clutching at the counter for support. "How could this happen? They released him from hospital. I spoke to him last night."

"Heart attacks happen, Sonya, despite everything," he said with a heavy heart. "This one has been waiting to happen, I'm afraid. We can't delay. I want you out of here."

"I can't stay anyway." She was clearly in great distress.

"No, you can't." His emotions were so strong he found himself speaking too harshly. "You have to shut up shop. I'll help you. You'll have to make it until further notice or bring in staff. That can be worked out. *You* won't be able to come back once the news breaks."

"I'm so sorry. So sorry," she moaned. "You think I killed him?" She had gone whiter than white. Her whole body was trembling. She was near enough to breaking.

"Don't torture yourself with thoughts like that," he said quickly. Whatever else he was, he wasn't a savage. No way could he pull her into his arms and offer comfort. His whole being was filled with guilt. "Marcus was a sick man."

"Where did he die?" She was trying desperately not to cry.

"Get yourself together, Sonya," he urged, his whole body tense. "His housekeeper found him. He died peacefully in his sleep."

"Thank God! Does Lady Palmerston know?"

"Sonya, *everyone* will know if we don't get a move on. I have to get you out of here. *I* have to get out of here. People know me. I fear this is going to be a very big story." He couldn't think of a worse scenario.

Over the coming days several photographs of Sonia appeared in the papers and on the Internet. In all of them she looked movie-star glamorous.

A real knockout was the general opinion. All of the photographs, on Marcus's arm—Marcus looking very much older—standing with David, the two of them appearing to be staring into one another's eyes, sitting at the table with the rich and famous as they had been on that gala night. The night she had been wearing a vintage evening gown and Lucille Wainwright's glorious emerald and diamond necklace with the diamond chandelier drops. Her expression in all of them was of cool grace, as if she were to the manner born.

Sonya knew, if no one else, she was the image of her mother, Lilla. Her mother in turn had inherited Katalin's remarkable looks and colouring. Such physical beauty was a gift of the genes.

In New York on a piercingly cold day Laszlo Andrassy-Von Neumann stood in complete silence in Central Park as a tall burly man wearing a greatcoat and a thick dark hat with ear flaps approached him. The man came to a brief halt, withdrawing a manila folder from a deep pocket. Andrassy-Von Neumann had already seen the photographs. They were unmistakably of a woman of his family. To his intense triumph the photographs were of his lost cousin, Sonya. A few more photographs had been taken on the street where she appeared to be in flight from the paparazzi, the rest were the same photographs that had been splashed across the Australian press.

So that was where young Sonya had sought sanctuary!

In exchange for the folder he passed his informant a thick envelope containing a substantial wad of money. It was worth every penny. He had now ascertained Sonya was living in Sydney, under the name of Erickson. It was an enormous stroke of luck the man she had been involved with had been a public figure, otherwise it might have taken longer to find her. She had covered her tracks like a professional. In a way he couldn't help but admire her. America had been very good to his family and him. But he was Hungarian. He wanted to get back to his roots. He had poured so much into his country of birth he now had the estate back: the palace, the title deeds, every last contract signed and sealed.

He was the Andrassy-Von Neumann heir. Katalin and Lilla were dead. He had, however, no real wish to harm Sonya. All she had to do was hand over the Madonna. He would make her an offer she couldn't refuse. Ten million into her bank account? That should do it. Of course, if she were foolish enough to hold out against him? He didn't believe she would. From a penniless little florist to a millionairess in one bound. Her grandmother and her mother and father were dead. He was certain she would see the good sense in making a deal. The *only* sense. After all, they were *family*. He was Count Laszlo Andrassy-Von Neumann. The title to his mind would never be defunct. And Sonya must never be allowed to lay claim to being a countess and the rightful heir of an ancient family's estates. She couldn't possibly stand a chance against him. Katalin's true identity had been destroyed. All reference to her dropped like the plague. Like her father, the old count who had been fool enough to remain in his palace, and her brother, the heir, Katalin had become a victim of war. As for her daughter, Lilla, she was the child of little more than a peasant. The extraordinary thing was he would have recognised his cousin Sonya anywhere. She was without question an Andrassy-Von Neumann.

The phone was ringing as Sonya let herself into the apartment. She was breathing hard with outrage. She had been chased home from a local convenience store by one of the TV channels, a car with a man and a woman in it, on the lookout for a few words, no doubt. It was pretty much like being a hunted animal.

"You have to get out of there."

It was David issuing instructions. He skipped the niceties. Niceties had flown out of the window.

"I'm not going anywhere, David," she said, resisting his formidable tone. "Those media hounds would be onto me wherever I went. Your parents are home?" A photograph of the Wainwrights arriving at the airport had already hit the front pages. No comment from either of them. Both had looked gravely upset.

He gave in to a maddened sigh. "Neither of them wants you at the funeral, Sonya."

"What about *you*, David?" she questioned, very intent on the answer. If he said he didn't want her there, she would begin immediately to try to banish him from her heart and mind.

"You have a right to be there," he said. "The problem, of course, is that your presence will cause a considerable stir."

"Too bad!" she answered coldly. "Marcus would have wanted me to be there. Marcus *loved* me. Have you forgotten?"

"Listen, Sonya, I'm desperately tired," he admitted, with a decided edge. "I maybe damned near thirty but my dad still likes to bawl me out. My mother too is good at beating a drum."

"So you have to go along with them? I understand." Her heart dropped like a stone.

"Oh, come off it!" he bit off. "I can take the heat. The whole business, you must admit, is ghastly. The press must be giving you hell?" He hadn't willed or wanted falling in love with this woman. But he had. He had a terrible longing to be with her. But he couldn't shake the crush of guilt. Or the knowledge he knew so little about her. She hadn't been given an opportunity to make a final decision. It was possible she could have actually accepted Marcus's proposal. Lack of trust was a sharp knife in his chest.

"The press are doing their level best," she told him, aware of his ambivalent feelings towards her. "No wonder celebrities hate them. The hounding is appalling."

"That's why I want you to shift. I have an apartment lined up for you. Somewhere very secure."

"Thank you, David," she said with icy politeness, "but I can't take advantage of your kind offer. I'm staying here. And I'm coming to the funeral. Your parents can bawl you out all they like. They can bawl me out too if they want to. I have backbone. I know enough about you to believe you're every bit as tough as your illustrious parents. I *can* promise you I'll keep a low profile. I won't do a thing to draw attention to myself."

His discordant laugh echoed down the phone. "Sonya, you must have learned by now you only have to show your face to draw attention."

"Did I ask to have this face?" she burst out angrily. "Blonde women get too much attention, all of us bimbos. We both know I intend to pay my last respects to Marcus. If your family thinks they can try any stand-over tactics, they won't work. I've known some truly *horrible* people, David. Your parents would be the good guys compared to them."

"Don't you worry the press will uncover these *horrible* people?" he warned her. "They're pursuing you, and they're going to keep it up. I would think Marcus has taken care of you in his will."

"What, you don't know *already*?" she asked witheringly.

"It's the waiting game." A stinging heat assailed him. He so wanted to see her, despite all that was happening. "Sonya, I want to help you. You need protection. You're going to be hotly pursued in the days ahead."

Pain shot through her right temple. A bad headache coming on. "That seems to be my fate, David, to be pursued. I'll say goodbye now. You must do what you have to do. I know you mean well, but I refuse to be deterred. I will be at Marcus's funeral. I don't intend to disguise myself either, like don a black wig. I am who I am."

"Then let's get your damned name right!" he retorted.

"That would be a big mistake!" She slammed down the phone.

One minute later she was in floods of tears.

She had met a man who was perfect to her. But all he wanted was to be rid of her.

CHAPTER SEVEN

SONYA had hoped the crowd would be so large she would have a good chance of slipping into the church unnoticed. As a necessary mark of respect to the Wainwright family she had done her best to look as inconspicuous as possible. Her giveaway white-blonde hair, she had all but concealed, fastening it in coils at the back, then topping it off with a wide-brimmed black hat. She had thought the inexpensive hat would be an excellent disguise. Unfortunately the result wasn't as low key as she had wished. The hat looked great on her. She already had a black dress and suitable accessories. Nothing ultra smart, but good quality. Part of the problem was, black suited her. It made a showcase of her colouring. Her hair wasn't on show, but she couldn't hide her white skin. But for this very sad occasion, black it had to be. She had no real status even if Marcus had given her that magnificent ring.

On and off for nights she had cried. She felt the tears coming now but she had to fight them back. She had to find and maintain her composure. A young woman in tears would only bring unwelcome attention. Mourners were everywhere. In its way it was a spectacular turnout. Among the dignitaries present, the State Premier, and a representative of the PM, who was out of the country. Marcus Wainwright had been a much respected man, a member of one of the richest and most influential families in the nation.

She made it up the stone steps on shaky legs and through the door of the cathedral. She looked to neither left nor right. A strong arm took hold of hers. She looked up quickly, anticipating trouble. What she saw was a heavily built man filling out a black suit. It was his job, she realized, to keep crowd control. He drew her aside. "Ms Erickson, isn't it?" he asked, very politely.

"Please take your hand off me," she said, keeping her tone low.

"You've done yourself no good coming here, miss." He was having difficulty not staring at her, she was so beautiful. "The family, I'm afraid, don't want you."

"I'm not here for the family, sir," Sonya said very quietly. "I'm here for Marcus Wainwright, my *dear* friend. Now, if you don't want me to raise my voice—I would regret the necessity, but I will—you'll take your hand away. Marcus would have wanted me here. Who do the other Wainwrights think they are, anyway?" Her green eyes flashed fire.

"Oh, they're Somebodies, Ms Erickson," he assured her, shaking his head. He could see the determination in her green eyes. He had to admire her for it. It was obvious he hadn't intimidated her in any way. Actually he didn't want to.

"Well, I'm a Somebody too," she said. "Please move away from me. I'm going to find a seat before they're all taken. I'll be as quiet as possible. I have no wish to cause offence but I refuse to be treated badly."

The security guard's eyes flickered. He dropped his arm and gave what came close to being a courteous bow. "Good luck to you, miss. I fear you're going to need it."

Every eye in the church turned as the Wainwright clan moved in procession to the front of the church. Sonya kept looking straight ahead. She couldn't see the casket. She didn't want to. She felt truly terrible. Three unimaginable things had happened. Marcus had fallen in love with her. Marcus was dead. David had accomplished what no other man had ever done. He had stolen her heart. Now he had as good as abandoned her. The service went on and on. She stood. She sat. She sang with the rest of them, not even knowing the words, but filling in as best she could. It was all so *unreal*. She listened to all the wonderful things family, close friends and dignitaries said about Marcus. David's contribution was the most beautiful and the most moving. She had to bite her lip hard the entire time he was speaking in his dark resonant voice. No one had dared mention the fact Marcus at the end of his life had been contemplating remarrying. The media wasn't any too sure of that. The Wainwright family was going to pretend she didn't exist.

Afterwards she stayed put until the church had almost been cleared before she made quietly for a side door, only to find the pathway outside had been blocked. That meant she had to go out of the front door. The Wainwrights, as was the custom, stood almost directly outside, receiving the long line of mourners who wished to express their sympathy. She would have to pass them. David was with them, tall, arresting and gravely formidable in his funereal clothes.

Looking straight in front of her, Sonya moved into the sunlight. It might have been a brilliant spotlight focused directly on her, because the buzz and hum of conversation among the huge crowd of mourners fell to a reverberating silence.

So much for the hat and the conservative clothes.

Her inner voice had kicked in.

Keep going. You can do it. Ignore all the curious and

*condemnatory faces. Ignore the Wainwrights. David is one
of them. Family solidarity is important. Think of yourself
as someone special. You are!*

She had herself under control, keeping her mind busy
with the thought of what the family might have done had
she been wearing Marcus's great diamond ring. Not only
that, *flashed* it. She still had the ring. David had refused
point blank to take charge of it, saying Marcus had wanted
her to have it and that was that. How exactly did she return
it? She was almost at the bottom of the stone steps when a
young woman chose that precise moment to approach her,
catching her by the arm.

Paula Rowlands moved right up into Sonya's face, mut-
tering in a low contemptuous voice, "The hide of you! I
don't believe it." She had been alerted Sonya was among
the mourners so, during the service while appearing to be
deeply saddened, she had decided on a strategy. She would
ambush this infuriating woman who had been told not to
show her face.

"Are you crazy?" Sonya asked. Disgust overcame any
sense of alarm. "Don't bother to answer that. I'd like you
to get away from me. And I mean *now*." She sounded far
more positive than she felt.

Neither young woman saw Holt Wainwright move
swiftly down the steps until he was towering over both
young women. "I'll take you to your car, Sonya," he said,
sounding as if he wouldn't tolerate any refusal. "You don't
intend to go on?"

Of course he meant to the cemetery. "No." She put his
mind at rest.

He turned his head to address Paula directly. His dark
eyes were as glittery as black crystals. "I had no idea, Paula,
you were so full of malice."

"Malice?" Deeply wounded, Paula stared up at him

incredulously. "*She's* the danger, Holt. *I'm* your friend, Holt, remember?"

"I'm trying to." He inclined his handsome head further towards her, still holding Sonya's arm. "Please do *not* offend my parents, Paula. Do *not* offend the memory of my uncle. Walk quietly away now."

Paula flushed scarlet. "Of course, Holt." She obeyed.

Those remaining of the huge crowd followed every step of their progress, across the road then down a side street to where Sonya had parked her car. That included press photographers and a television camera, although they'd had the common decency to keep their distance at this point.

"You were cruel to her, weren't you?" Sonya said on a distressed breath, but very glad of his supporting arm.

His handsome face was closed. "She deserved it. What was she saying anyway?"

"What you'd expect. Do *you* think I have a hide, David?"

"I think you've got a lot of guts," he answered tersely. "Not too many people stand up to my parents."

"*You* do. Otherwise you wouldn't be here with me now. Or this is one of your strategies? Get her away as quickly and as quietly as possible."

He could see her hurt. It registered in her beautiful eyes. Nothing but distress for the both of them. "All you need to know is *this*, Sonya. I won't have anyone attacking you. Whether it would have turned out well or a disaster, Marcus loved you."

"So you went for disaster? I guess you're with me now for Marcus's sake?"

"Sonya, right now I'm here for *you*." They had reached her small car, the roof and the bonnet lightly scattered with tiny yellow flowers from the overhead trees. "I need to talk to you, Sonya," he said.

He appeared to be studying every separate feature of her face.

"You're going straight home?"

"No, I'm taking off for parts unknown." She offered a dismal joke.

"Maybe that would be a good idea for a week or two." His forehead creased in concentration.

"So where do you suggest I go? Far North Queensland. Cape York?" She named a remote part of Queensland a few thousand miles away. "Or maybe across Bass Strait to Tasmania. That should be far enough."

"I can arrange Port Douglas." He named a famous Queensland beach resort. The aching hunger he felt for her was squeezing his chest.

"Problem is I'm not a sun worshipper like you. I'll think of something, David. I can see you're anxious to get rid of me."

He didn't deign to answer. *God, what do I do now?*

"Sonya Erickson, the girl who can't be found." She unlocked her car, sweeping the offending hat off her head and throwing it onto the seat. Then she shook her head, shaking her hair free of its tight, confining pins.

"How could you expect me to trust you, when you don't trust me, Sonya? You've told me nothing. At best you've thrown out a few clues. What could be so bad you keep it locked up? *Who* is looking for you, Sonya?" His tone was deadly serious. "Someone is. I'm convinced Erickson isn't your real name."

"I don't have a name," she said mournfully. No reason to tell him now. "I'm like my maternal grandmother. My identity has been lost."

He stared down at her, the waterfall of hair, her marvellous illuminated skin. "That doesn't make sense."

"It makes sense to me," she said.

"The will is going to be read this afternoon," he offered abruptly. "You're in it.'

"You're certain of that?" she asked scornfully. "So where am I—top of the list? Or second? God forbid I should rob you of your inheritance."

"Just once, Sonya. Be *yourself.*"

"Good heavens, David. You sound as though you care?" She knew she had reached a crisis point in her life. She had to be strong. "If Marcus did remember me in his will I'm sure it'll be contested. This woman has exerted undue pressure on an ailing man might be the way to go." She knew she sounded bitter, but she had to make a final break.

"Marcus wouldn't have wasted any time seeing you were provided for," he said. God knew that would cause, not ripples, but a flood.

"Aren't the Wainwrights going to love that?" she scoffed.

Only her lovely mouth was quivering. Her desire to turn him away was in vain. "It's not the money, Sonya."

"Of course it's the money!" she said angrily, fighting tears. "Even billionaires don't knock back money. Money is everything to them. If Marcus has left me money I can refuse it. Or, better yet, give it away. Anyway, you could be *wrong.*"

He very much doubted that. "I want to see you this evening," he said, tension in his entire body. "I can tell you then."

"But I don't want to see you." She slipped behind the wheel with natural grace, her eyes glittering with tears.

He looked in at her. "Yes, you *do.*" Love was the best or the worst of spells. Once under it, one lost sight of common sense, even reason.

Sonya drove away without another word. On the one hand she believed she had Laszlo's people looking for her.

The big worry was her recent notoriety. She had never appeared in a newspaper before. She was exposed as never before. On the other hand, the Wainwrights, and their extended family, were all involved in some way in Wainwrights' numerous enterprises. They were the ones who wanted to slam the door in her face. David was powerfully attracted to her. She knew that just as she knew he didn't trust her. Who could blame him? She was acting as though she had a disreputable past and in some ways she had. She knew he was feeling a degree of guilt. She was feeling it too. When they had come together no thoughts of Marcus had stood in the way. She recognised too powerful parents had a way of having the last word.

Better you'd never come into his life.

Nor he into hers.

Every Wainwright face showed shocked disbelief. They were all gathered in the library while the family solicitor read out the will. Holt sat between his mother and father, from time to time taking his mother's hand. She might not be showing it, but he knew she was deeply shocked by Marcus's sudden death.

Charities dear to Marcus's heart were treated very generously, so too young members of the family. There were bequests to lifelong friends, tidy sums to staff present and past, Marcus's collection of valuable paintings—three of the most important to the National Art Gallery, the remainder to his mother, along with the bronze sculptures she had long admired. Chinese porcelains, jades and ivories went to Rowena, who was too upset to attend the will reading. A great windfall of shares went to his father, Robert, and many personal effects. The bulk of his uncle's fortune, including a hefty block of shares from Marcus's large portfolio went to him. Nothing unexpected about that. All the family knew he had been the apple of his uncle's eye. However, to everyone's stunned amazement twenty million dollars went to a Sonya Erickson, an unknown, for whom in Marcus's words he had, "a great affection".

His father and mother showed no emotion whatever throughout, but he could see his mother's cheeks were flushed and his father's strong jaw set. There was going to be a huge fuss later. Who *was* this Sonya Erickson?

"One thing," Sharron Holt-Wainwright said tersely. "She's very beautiful, very classy."

His mother never missed anything.

Everyone had gone home, most in a state of shock, to thrash out the ramifications of the will in private. Twenty million dollars to some young florist? She could buy a whole rainforest.

"Pour me a whisky and water, would you, David?" His father was down, down, down. The brothers had been very close.

"I'll have one as well," said his mother, who looked similarly drained. "I take a very dim view of all this." She looked across the room at her son. "How did this all happen, Holt? Surely you could have intervened in some way? It seems a terrible thing to say of darling Marcus, but he must have temporarily lost his mind. She's young enough to have been his daughter."

"Maybe he wanted a daughter," Robert Wainwright suggested. "Poor old Marcus was terribly lonely, no matter how hard we tried to bolster his spirits. He missed Lucy so. David, you're looking doubtful?"

"Marcus gave her a ring," Holt, well used to his parents using both names for him, responded bluntly. He handed a crystal tumbler to each of them. They would have to know. "An engagement ring."

"Good God!" Robert Wainwright's dark head fell back against the leather chair, as though for once he felt defeated.

"What can have been in Marcus's head?" his mother wailed. "He's been chased by plenty of women these past years. Suitable women his own age."

"He didn't *want* a woman his own age," David told her dryly. "He wanted Sonya."

"One needn't wonder why," Sharron said in a voice dry as ash. "Twenty million will make a big difference to a working girl."

"She doesn't know she's a rich woman yet," David said.

"A *very* rich woman." Robert Wainwright gave a hard cynical bark. "A woman as beautiful as that could wind any man around her little finger. We have to meet this girl, David. Make an effort to avoid any unpleasantness. At least she won't need to sell her story to some vapid woman's magazine. Not *now*. She's a florist?"

"Does she intend to return the ring or is she going to keep it as a souvenir?" Sharron asked, with heavy sarcasm.

"She did try to give it into my care."

"And?" Sharron fired up, staring back very closely at her son.

"I didn't take it," he replied flatly. "Marcus gave it to her. He wanted her to have it."

"It's the rare woman who gives anything back," said his father. "You must arrange some time for us to meet her."

"So does she just drop in or what?" He gave vent to a burst of anger.

His mother continued to stare at him. "Invite her to dinner," she said eventually. "I think my judgment might be more reliable than dear Marcus's. Or even *yours*, my darling. Make it this coming Saturday evening. I'm determined to get answers from this girl. If she's as smart as I think she is, she'll come. She must be made to understand no one trifles with this family."

It was a simple matter to follow his target back from the funeral of the bigwig she was alleged to have been involved with. A nice enough apartment complex, but nothing to speak about. Of course, she had been lying low. The count was certain she had no money to speak of. What she did have was a treasured icon that rightfully belonged to the count. It was his job to get it back. He could not fail. He would not fail. The count did not tolerate failure. He would keep her under surveillance, and then select the right moment. He was to offer her a great deal of money in exchange for the icon and her word that she would abandon any claim to the Andrassy-Von Neumann estate. There was to be no violence. Violence was a last resort. In the girl's place he would jump at the count's offer. The irony was she could have easily passed for the count's own granddaughter. The family resemblance was very strong.

CHAPTER EIGHT

HOLT arrived at Sonya's apartment around seven-thirty p.m., parking his borrowed car outside the building. His top-of-the-line Mercedes would be something of a give-away and he didn't want that. His nerves were strung tight. No way could he possibly *act* the way he felt. He was a man under considerable constraint. A man who was head over heels in love with a young woman his uncle had asked to be his wife. Moreover one neither of them had known much about. Now Marcus was no longer with them and he was left torn by feelings of guilt as though he had committed some serious transgression. It was largely irrational but it was there all the same. He felt the crush of it in his chest.

Today had been one of the worst days of his life. It took all his self control not to allow it to descend into chaos. Sonya, Ice Princess that she was, had been affected too. She could even feel some of his guilt. They had been caught up together, filled with a mad, uncaring rapture. There was even a possibility she mightn't want to see him again. Especially when she found out she was a very rich young woman. Real life beat fiction hands down, he thought.

She opened the door to him looking anything but an adventuress. Indeed she looked young and innocent. He took in at a glance the absence of her normal cool composure and the tantalising veil of sophistication. Her beautiful hair was hanging down her back in a thick plait, like a schoolgirl. The lovely colour was gone from her face. Her skin was as white as the petals of a rose. She was wearing a soft loose violet dress with some sparkly embroidery around the oval neckline and the long hem.

The opposite of the elation was despair. He wanted her so badly the pain was almost too fierce to be borne. But Marcus's sudden death had brought the barriers down. Could they ever come up? Suddenly, passionately, he reached for her hand. Their fingers entwined with a life of their own.

"Sonya, how are you?"

"Very shaky." She made no movement to pull away, though the shadow of Marcus loomed large.

There are rules, rules, rules. Self-esteem demands you stick to the rules.

What rules? She had discovered she had two inner voices. They went back and forth. Both in conflict. One haunted her in the early hours, castigating her for her inaction. The other told her she had made no positive commitment to Marcus. It was Marcus who had acted as though the relationship *he* had wanted were carved in stone. If she was to blame in any way—and she believed she was—it had been her inability to keep their friendship within bounds. The result, Marcus had steamed ahead with their friendship at the rate of knots. Fine man that he had been, Marcus had lived a life where he truly could have just about anything he wanted. The trade off for her was, he would give her a life of great privilege and comfort.

David's voice broke into her troubled thoughts.

"Have you eaten?"

"I'm not really hungry. Have you?" She risked staring up into his brilliant dark eyes. He was beyond handsome. But she registered his immense strain.

Such a short period of time since he had seen her, yet it felt like an eternity.

"I said have you eaten?" Sonya repeated, knowing he hadn't properly heard her.

He shook his dark head. "We could go out. On the other hand, we'd better stay in. I didn't even bring my own car. I stole one."

"You *didn't*!" She led him into the living room.

"Well, I took it without asking." He tried for a smile, but it was too much of an effort. Despondently he slumped onto one of the sofas.

"I could make us a sandwich," she offered, thinking she too could break under the pressure. He looked marvellous to her in the bright lights, his coal-dark eyes glittering in his finely sculpted face. "It won't take any time."

"Take all the time you like." He was daunted by the strength of his feelings for her. He knew he shouldn't be here. Not feeling like this. "How are you doing *really*?" he asked.

"I don't know." She moved into the galley kitchen. Her answer was very quiet. He had never thought to see her so subdued. "It all seems like a bad dream. I wanted Marcus in my life. But not as a husband, as my friend. Now I feel like I've somehow betrayed him."

He set his jaw. Didn't he share her feelings? "It wouldn't have worked, Sonya, even if the two of us hadn't become involved. I take the blame. I acted upon the attraction. Only Marcus didn't want you for a friend. He wanted you for a wife. You're telling me the truth? The relationship hadn't become sexual?"

She flared up so quickly, warmth rushed back into her body. "Think what you like!"

He sat forward, putting two hands to his dark head. "Sonya, I'm sick of *thinking*." He laid it out for her.

She could see the intolerable stress. It caused her to come from behind the counter. "I *told* you, David," she said in a calmer voice. "We're both upset. You've been with your parents, haven't you?"

"Of course I've been with my parents." His reply was decidedly edgy. "The will was read late this afternoon."

"Tell me you got the lion's share," she invited, hoping that was true.

"I did," he said, glancing up at her, desire pumping into him no matter what. "*You* got twenty million dollars."

"What?" She registered the steely expression on his face. The next moment she was overtaken by dizziness. "Twenty—" she began, then broke off. Oxygen wasn't reaching her brain. Her legs were starting to give. She told herself dazedly she had never fainted in her life, even when times were very bad, but the room was filling up with clouds of grey smoke.

David moved so fast he was near flying. He grabbed her before she hit the floor. "Sonya!" He felt intense anger at himself. Was he ever going to stop putting her to the test? He could at least have worked up to telling her of her inheritance, only he'd wanted her spontaneous reaction. Shame all around him. For what he had here was a genuine faint.

He arranged her on the rug that lay beneath her feet. Lying down was the fastest way to recovery. As a yachts-man, he had taken all the necessary first-aid courses. Anyone could faint given the right conditions. This was shock. Her eyes were open. She hadn't lost full conscious-ness. It was what was called a pre-syncope. He found it simple to diagnose. She was frowning as if irritated. After a moment she tried to sit up, but he held her down, grab-bing a cushion off the sofa and putting it beneath her head.

"It's okay, Sonya. Lie there for a while. You'll be right in a moment or two."

It was all his fault. Angry with himself, he lowered himself onto the rug beside her, lying back. He was fed up with everything. Fed up with running the gauntlet of emotions. For a man who had been in control of his world he was floundering badly. He was thankful at least he hadn't *slept* with Sonya. Only, in kissing her with Marcus in the background, he felt as though he had given into a passion that had somehow diminished him. Betrayal wasn't in his nature. He had truly loved his uncle. Only he had wanted Sonya more.

You still want her.

His inner voice forced him to own up.

Neither of them spoke. Neither of them knew what to say. That was the full irony of it. They just lay there, side by side, each locked in their own thoughts that were remarkably similar.

Finally Sonya said, "I can't handle this, David. It's all too much. I don't want Marcus's money. A gift, a memento, maybe, I would have accepted, but never a fortune! I can't live with a gesture like that. I wasn't going to marry him."

"You're sure about that?" Jealousy exploded out of him. How ignoble!

She made a little keening sound, struggling not to turn to him.

Only David was compelled to turn to her. "Okay, I'm sorry. I didn't mean that."

"It will happen again," she told him bleakly. "Your efforts to bring me down."

"Or wait for you to bring *me* down," he said with black humour. "One of my fears is I know so little about you, Sonya. You have to accept Marcus's legacy. You can't give it back. No one will contest your right to have it. It was Marcus's wish."

"It's *my* wish he hadn't." How could he understand her, when she couldn't understand herself? From the age of sixteen she'd had no one close to advise her; no one to help her through her traumas, her never-ending grief at what had happened to her parents. Hadn't there been enough tragedy in their family life? What relatives she had, overnight changed. They wanted only to possess her, use her. Her heart had been cracked so badly she had thought it beyond repair. Yet under Marcus's benign influence, the mending had begun. But it was David who had brought her back to full blazing life.

"People will hate me," she said.

He answered quietly enough. "I thought you didn't care about what people thought?"

"It seems I was wrong. I'm ready to get up." From feeling unnaturally chilled, her blood was heating up. She knew the sensations for what they were: an automatic response to his nearness. They had always had this dynamic from the moment they met. There was small comfort in the fact neither of them had engineered a relationship. The only thing to blame was fate.

"Why bother?" The slightest trace of humour crept into his voice. "I'm liking it here." Compulsively, he reached out a long arm to put it beneath her head. So close to, he was inhaling her natural sweet fragrance like an aphrodisiac. "What am I going to do with you, Sonya?"

"What do you *want* to do with me?" There was a complete absence of provocation in her voice.

Yet it threw him into a kind of panic. "What I've wanted to do since I laid eyes on you," he said, feeling he was moving beyond all pretence.

"That *cannot* happen, David. You have lost your beloved uncle. I have lost a true friend." She continued to lie quietly beside the lean, splendid length of him. "What did your parents have to say?"

"They want to meet you, of course."

Her breath fluttered. "They want to find out exactly what kind of person I am? How did I scheme to get Marcus to fall in love with me?" She was too saddened for any show of indignation.

"Something like that," he said sombrely.

"Did you tell them he gave me an engagement ring?"

"I told them you tried to give it back into my keeping. I refused to take it."

"So they have serious business to attend to," she concluded. "They need to check this Sonya Erickson out?"

"*Someone* needs to, Sonya," he said bluntly. "I've told you, if there's anything worrying you, anything that could be called a problem, you'd be wise to tell me now."

She stared up at the white ceiling. "Perhaps you are overestimating your importance in my life, David. I am now an heiress, am I not?"

He gave a hard little grunt. "Yes, you are, but it doesn't help anyone when you spend your time trying to put me off. Don't you realize that? It's all going to come out, Sonya," he assured her with some force. "This legacy Marcus left you. It will be the talk of the town. Someone always spills the beans, no matter how many times they're told to keep their mouths shut. Your legacy far exceeds anything the minor beneficiaries received. People look to motivation, reasons. Why would a man like Marcus leave a young woman he knew for only a short time a small fortune?'

"*Small?*" she exclaimed in disbelief. "Twenty million dollars is *small*?"

"Well, it's hardly *big*!"

It was difficult to believe he was serious. Yet she knew he was. There was a *universe* of difference between them. She sat up, willing the strength to return to her legs. "So now I see you for exactly *who* you are. You're David Wainwright, heir to a great fortune."

"You're missing the bit about the huge responsibilities that go with it," he said bluntly. "No one talks about *them*. My father has always been under tremendous pressure. I am *now*. I expect a lot more in the future. It's not just a question of having a lot of money, Sonya. It's holding onto it for future generations. And I would remind you my family, through the Wainwright Foundation, does a lot of good."

"So I stand corrected. I think it might be a good idea if you left." Anger that could not be totally explained was a burning, smouldering trail towards dynamite. "Is it okay I get past you? Or do I have to go over the top of you?" Such sensations were coursing through her body, they were making her a little crazy.

He gave a deep groan, "God, yes, *do it*!" he invited.

"Maybe I will! You should not test me in this way." She began to lever her body over his.

It was a huge mistake.

His grip on her was so hard and strong his hands might have been made out of steel. "Why not? I'm not going to make it easy for you." The protective walls were imploding. A hunger more savage than anything he had ever known welled up inside him. He held her in place over his aroused body, then, when she moaned, he reversed their positions so he was half atop her, taking most of his weight on his upper arms.

"In one way I wish you hadn't done that," he said, staring into her emerald eyes, "and then again, I'm so glad you did."

"Always *my* fault?" Desire had all but knocked the breath out of her.

"Of course it's your fault," he mocked. "The little games you play." He displayed the strength and grace of a gymnast, holding his own weight while dropping taunting little kisses all over her face, her mouth, the line of her jaw and the length of her throat. Then he came back to run the tip of his tongue over the outline of her full mouth, tracing its contours.

It made her head spin. She wanted to pull him down on top of her. Press herself into him. Revel in the weight of his body on hers. She wasn't strong enough to withstand the tongues of flame licking at her. The little moans she kept hearing, pathetically, were hers. Her back was arching off the floor, her yearnings painfully clear. The stabbing sensations between her legs had become pain. At long last she was totally awakened to passion. Worse, her body, regardless of her mind, was demanding consummation.

"You're so…beautiful," he murmured.

It sounded as if he lamented the fact. His kisses, though long and deep, were taunting in their fashion. He *knew* she was desperate for more of him. She knew it as she knew his feelings of guilt. She shared them. Had dear, kind Marcus actually poisoned any hope of anything *real* between them? There was such turbulence in the air it was crowding the tiny space of common sense that remained in her head.

Don't let him know just how desperately you yearn for him. Don't do it. You will never meet his needs or the Wainwright expectations.

"How do I stop kissing you?" he muttered against her throat. "Is there a way?"

"You could let me up." She felt feverish with excitement, yet she found sufficient strength to speak coldly.

"I don't *want* to let you up. *Ever!*"

"Even when I want to be free?"

His answer cut to the truth. "You weren't free from the moment you looked into my eyes. Your will is falling short of your desires, Sonya," he mocked her.

"As is yours." She gave a broken laugh. "I thought, as you're always telling me, David, I'm expert at concealing myself?"

"It's high time we settled that. How many other men have kissed you?" He couldn't resist suckling her full lower lip. It was aquiver, so soft and lush.

"My father, long dead," she confessed, in a strange off-key whisper.

That sobered him. She had never mentioned her father. "Sonya, you must tell me about him." He swung back onto the floor, staring down at her, with such intensity in his eyes surely she would respond.

Only she didn't. "Let me up, David," she ordered.

"Certainly, my lady." He stood, drawing her to her feet, but keeping a steadying arm around her. He was acutely aware of the trembling in her body. He understood. *He* was a million miles away from being calm himself. "Why don't you lie on the sofa?" he suggested. "I won't bother you. I'll sit here." He pulled out an armchair. "You must talk, Sonya."

"It's rather terrible, the gift of love," she mused. She didn't take the sofa; she sat straight. "Rapture on the one hand. The real possibility it will be taken away on the other. In my experience love has meant loss. I'm not talking romantic love. I've shielded myself from that. I thought it wise. I have not been open with you and others, because I've found it so difficult to surrender my trust, David. Do you believe in heaven?" She looked at him, her heart in her eyes.

"If I did, Marcus will be there." Grief showed on his handsome face.

"So you don't?"

"One needs a whole lot of *faith*, Sonya. Faith is believing in something for which there's no proof. I keep an open mind on a possible afterlife. That's all."

"My parents were very good people," she said, looking down at her locked hands. "My grandmother. They believed in heaven."

"Do *you*?"

She arranged her thick plait over her shoulder. "How can I? Again, in my experience it's the good people who die. Bad people prosper."

"And the bad people are?" He kept his eyes trained on her, hoping her practised composure was about to crack open.

"My family."

"Family?" He frowned, thoroughly perplexed, but he stayed quiet. If he stayed quiet she might confide in him. David sat back in his chair, staring across at her.

She didn't speak again for a full minute. Her reticence was so well ingrained.

"Sonya, my parents want to meet you," he prompted her. "They'd like to ask you some questions. Surely you agree they're entitled to some answers? Marcus was my father's brother. They were very close. My mother loved Aunt Lucille. Marcus had asked you to be his wife. He gave you a magnificent ring. They know about that as they have to."

The emerald of her eyes darkened. "I tried to give it back."

"So where is it?" He suddenly thought to ask. "Valuable things need safekeeping."

A madness got into her. "You want to see something

to surpass your precious emeralds?" A blaze of challenge came into her face, her beautiful eyes flashed.

"So show me," he invited, wondering what this was all about.

"Wait and see." She sprang up, rushing down the corridor.

Moments later, she was back, holding something in her hands. A small book of some sort? he thought. An old photograph in a very unusual leather-bound case, dark green, gold-tooled. She sat down beside him breathing with enormous excitement. "You may look." She passed the case to him with very real reverence.

It was oddly heavy for its size and it had a tangible aura. It also gave off an aroma like woody incense. There were sparkling tears in her eyes.

"Sonya!" He set the case down a moment to stare at her. "Whatever *is* this?" There was such a look on her face it would make a strong man weep.

"Open it."

It was a command.

He didn't attempt any levity. He knew it would be a huge mistake. But as he took the case into his hands he felt a strange tingling. It ran up his arms, like shivers of electricity, and struck a chord in his body. He even had to bunch his hands. "What am I holding—a relic of some sort?" He knew she was deeply religious. Her background, of course.

"Come, open it." Her hand fell imperiously on his arm. "I have guarded it with my life."

She sounded *tortured*.

"Sonya, I'll do everything I can to help you." He felt such a protective surge she could surely feel it? "Are you in trouble?"

"David, I didn't *steal it*," she told him, almost kindly.

He released a breath. "Thank God for that!"

Two sides of the case opened out, like a triptych. Very carefully, as though he was handling something precious and very rare, he opened one side, and then the other.

He possessed a good *eye*, refined as it was, growing up surrounded by beautiful things. Still he had to gasp, "God, is this *real*?" He was staring down in stunned amazement at what was an extremely old and valuable, if not priceless, icon of the Madonna.

"Not God, the Madonna," she announced, leaning into his shoulder.

Whatever scenarios he had imagined, it was never this. "But this is *extraordinary*! You must tell me about it." The Madonna's headdress and robe, the framing all around the icon, the ornamentation on both sides, were studded with precious stones—diamonds, rubies, sapphires, emeralds— and embellished with seed pearls. The halo around the Madonna's head was gold leaf. Her crown, studded with diamonds, had the unmistakable gleam of twenty-four-carat gold. The expression on the beautiful Byzantine face was mournful. The Madonna was not carrying The Child.

He shot her a piercing glance. "Are you sure some museum isn't after this as we speak? For pity's sake, Sonya, if *you* didn't steal it, and I believe you, did someone close to you?" Surely one wasn't allowed to carry a precious icon out of whatever country it came from, he thought. Poland, Hungary? It was obviously Roman Catholic.

"Be certain of it, David," she said, with a proud lift of her chin. "It was *not* stolen. The icon has been in my family for centuries. It was the only thing my grandmother could spirit out of Hungary in 1945 when the Russians were advancing." Her voice broke. She gave a little choking sob, which she quelled in an instant.

"Sonya, you've stunned me with this," he said slowly,

even if it did explain so much about her. "I regret I've sometimes taunted you about your aristocratic connections. Now it appears you have them. Could you tell me your grandmother's story? It sounds important."

She sank back against the sofa. "I don't share my secret with anyone," she said. "Now there is *you*." She began to speak in what seemed to him a trancelike voice. "My maternal grandmother's name was Katalin Andrassy-Von Neumann. She was the only one to escape the Russians under the protection of a family servant. My great-grandfather, Count Andrassy-Von Neumann, and Katalin's older brother, Matthias, remained at the palace. My great-grandfather's brother, Karoly, got together as much of his fortune as he could, then fled with his family to the United States. They all survived and became very rich. Maybe a lot richer than the Wainwrights." She shrugged ironically. "The Russians captured my great-grandfather and Matthias. They were never seen or heard of again. My grandmother lived the remainder of her life in far away Norway. She was forced into marriage with a member of the loyal servant's family after the old man died. My mother was married off too. She managed to escape. She found her saviour in my father. He was Austrian, of good family and thus a man of influence. I never knew the icon existed until I was sixteen. Not long after that, my parents were killed in a car crash." She stopped abruptly.

"Are you okay?" He spoke very quietly, concerned for her, but anxious not to stop the flow.

"Why not?" She gave a discordant laugh. "I'm speaking to you, aren't I? It is costing me an effort."

"I can see that. Sonya, I'm so sorry. We can stop now if you want to." It didn't seem right to upset her further.

Only she took up her story. "I am an orphan of the storm. I will go to my grave believing the crash that killed my parents was engineered by my cousin, Laszlo. He now calls himself Count Laszlo Andrassy-Von Neumann, though he is not entitled to." She was speaking with outright contempt. "I never feel safe even in this country of peace and freedom where everyone says exactly what they please. I *need* to feel safe, David."

"So you thought you would have been safe with Marcus?"

"He had so much to offer," she said mournfully. "I'm not talking about his money. I mean his kindness, his generosity, his protective feelings towards me. I wanted to let him into my life eventually. Only I found I couldn't marry a man I did not love in the romantic fashion. My feeling for Marcus was not like that. He would have been so perfect as the uncle I had long wished for."

He readily saw that. "Humour me, won't you? Start again and go slowly. Tell me about this Laszlo character. Where does he live?"

"Not here." She shuddered. "He has vast interests in the United States and in Hungary. The estate has been returned to him as the rightful heir along with many of the stolen paintings and so forth. He divides his time between the United States, a country so good to his father and him, and Hungary. He is Hungarian through and through. He wants the Madonna."

Why wouldn't he? "This is quite a story." Indeed his eyes were dazzled by the glitter given off by the many precious stones that decorated the icon. And Sonya had had it in her possession all this time. "One to marvel over really. Princess Michael of Kent and her mother took refuge here in Australia. Quite a few Jewish families, once immensely rich, came here to live out the rest of their shattered lives. Marcus knew one such lady. A great lady, he always said."

"Many European and Russian families have such stories," she said. "I should tell you Laszlo never does anything himself. He has people to carry out his wishes; do all his dirty work. He wasn't even in Germany when my parents were killed. The authorities said it was an accident. I *know* my mother went in fear of Laszlo. I can't talk any more about this." She bent her shining head.

"I'm grateful for what you have said, Sonya. It explains so much. But surely with all his resources this Laszlo was able to make contact with you?"

"Track me down, don't you mean?" She gazed at him, her eyes matching the glitter of the emeralds.

"Well—yes."

"He hasn't so far," she said. "I've been extremely careful. I train myself well. Who would think a young woman who worked in a florist shop would have a priceless icon in her possession anyway? Why should I be poor when I could be rich? Some people, heathens, might even pry out the stones. They would be worth a fortune. But that would be sacrilege. The icon remains with me. *I* am the rightful heir. Not Laszlo. I know it. He knows it."

There was big trouble brewing here, David thought. Sonya had long been under cover, but now that cover was blown. Ironically through her connection with his family. It was his family who now bore the responsibility of protecting her. "I think you should get out of this apartment," he said, decisively.

She faced him directly. *"No!"*

"Then you're not thinking straight," he told her, tersely. "You've had considerable exposure in the press. No country on earth is isolated these days. Our own press will be trying to find out all they can about you. *I* made an attempt that came to nothing. But it will all change. What is your *real* name?"

She smiled ironically into his eyes. "It matters?"

"Of course it matters." He spoke sternly, in an effort to get through to her.

"So, would you believe Von Neumann? I am Sonya Von Neumann. My father's family had connections with the Andrassy-Von Neumanns. That's how my mother met my father."

"Then surely after the tragedy there was some member of his family to protect you?" Even now he knew she wasn't giving him her complete trust.

"Never to *protect* me," she said with some bitterness. "To take me over. Control me. Marry me off to one of them. That wasn't going to happen. My grandmother was the heir, the only one remaining. She died. Next in line, my mother. You know her story. Now *me*. I am Countess Andrassy-Von Neumann under the old system, now defunct. Laszlo is *not* the count, but he doesn't care. He calls himself that. *Ergo*, it is!"

He frowned in concentration. "So tell me, Sonya, what is it *you* want? You obviously haven't resolved your burning issues. Is it your plan to oust your cousin? Are you now thinking of starting proceedings that could cost millions of dollars and drag on for years? You might have inherited real money from Marcus, but from what you tell me Laszlo is a very rich man with far greater resources to fight you. Most likely if he's poured money into the country of his birth he will have support in high places."

She sank small pearly teeth into her lower lip. "This I know. I can't fight him. I'd like to if only to prove he does not have a legitimate claim. It could take years out of my life. I don't want to go back to Hungary. I am happy here. He *is* family. He is male. I know he will have done everything in his power to restore the estate. He can even call himself the count. But he cannot have the Andrassy Madonna. That is *mine*!"

"But you fear he wants it very badly?"

"He wants it with a passion," she declared, very passionate about it herself. "It is supposed to have great spiritual powers. Laszlo holds himself to be head of the family. The family icon should be in *his* possession. The monetary value of the icon is not of importance to him, although it would be near priceless. The Madonna was always regarded as the family's most treasured possession."

He sat back. "And where exactly do you keep this priceless possession? Don't for God's sake tell me at the back of a drawer?"

"I am not going to say anything further."

"No, you're rather foolishly going to go back into your shell," he said shortly, pinning her narrow wrist. "You don't trust me?"

"I am not going to tell you," she repeated, sounding driven. "And you can give your parents a message. I will not be interrogated."

It took an effort to keep his tone level. "You need help, Sonya," he said quietly. "If you can only say so much to me, maybe you could speak to a professional? You've had to keep far too much bottled up. You've had to harden your heart."

"I didn't do such a good job with you," she pointed out with some hostility. "I try to not think of you but you get closer and closer."

"It works both ways, Sonya," he said, holding onto her. "I held my uncle very dear."

"And I did not?" She was suddenly furious. "Maybe you think I am telling you a fairy story?"

He held her stormy gaze. "The icon makes it real.

Everything about you falls into place. It must have been really bad living with the constant fear of discovery?"

She relaxed very slightly. "Laszlo had my parents killed. He will pay."

How? he wondered. "You could go public," he offered a suggestion with feigned seriousness. "You could never confront him yourself. Did you think that's where Marcus could step in?"

"No, no!" She shook her head. "Marcus was for protection. Laszlo will move heaven and earth to find me if he learns I'm here in Australia. He has dangerous people he can and will use."

"Not with me and my family in your life," he assured her. "Just tell me this. Could someone find the icon if they searched this place thoroughly? A professional, not a common or garden thief."

She swallowed. "They would have to be very, very good."

"Get real, Sonya!" he exclaimed. "If Lazlo sent someone he or she would be very, very good. That's why we need to get you out of here."

"To where, David?" she asked, clearly agitated. "Join you at your apartment? Join you in your bed?"

"You can stop that right now," he said. "Has anyone ever tried to force sex on you, Sonya? Someone in the past?"

"Men can be cruel!" she said.

He groaned, afraid of what she might explain. "Some are. Most aren't."

"The answer you require is *no*. I am—and you are hearing *correctly*—a virgin."

For a long moment he couldn't formulate a word. Was she telling the truth? She was an extremely beautiful young woman, twenty-five, but she did have that touch-me-not air. "I don't know if I should believe you," he said slowly. "How could you escape a love affair or two?"

"So?" She tilted her chin, looking at him disdainfully. "Twenty-five is good to be a virgin. I'll give myself only to the man I love."

He released a stifled breath. "Sonya, in my own defence I have to point out you've behaved like a very passionate young woman with me. Marcus wanted you to be his wife. Did you tell *him* you were a virgin?"

"None of his business," she said. "*My* business. I don't care if I *never* have sex."

He raised his hands in a gesture that said, *Enough!* "You'd better start learning to handle the truth. We've come pretty close to crossing the line."

"All right, I admit it!" Tears filled her eyes. "I wasn't looking for any of this. It just happened. I wish I could say I was a normal person, like your girlfriends. Paula Rowlands, however, is an exception. I am *not* normal. Because I have not had a normal life. I've lived with too much fear. I've lived with being greatly desired. For *sex*! There, now you know! Not *me*, who I am. My face, my body. Like my mother in her first disastrous marriage. But I was to be allowed time. I was the chosen one, always watched. I was a prize, you see. I was treated well in some ways. I wasn't beaten or starved or locked up. These were civilised people of good family. The intimidation was subtle but very real. I knew I had to escape after one frightening encounter. So I did."

He felt so greatly perturbed, he moved to cradle her in his arms. "These people, these relatives, have much to answer for. Did they by any chance know about the Madonna?"

She shook her head. "Of course not! They all believed it was lost along with so many other treasures. *I* was the treasure. The sixteen-year-old. So pretty! A pretty woman is always desirable, is she not?"

"Pretty doesn't say it," he said. "You had the money to run?"

"I did. Not a great amount, but enough to eventually get out of Europe. My father died without making a will, you see. He didn't know he was destined to die early. The money, of course, would have come to me in time, when I was eighteen, but meanwhile I had a guardian. It was the guardian who wanted me. He too was all of thirty years older."

"And he didn't come after you?" His voice hardened at the thought. Sixteen, robbed of her parents, and under tremendous fear of sexual abuse.

"I told you. I'm good at disappearing. I had protection. I had my father's gun."

He was surprised by how much that shocked him. "There are strict gun laws in the country, Sonya. Do you still have it?"

"Of course not!" she answered scornfully. "I threw it in a river as soon as I felt safe. I couldn't get into this country with a gun in my luggage. Guns are terrible things."

"I'm so glad you agree. Sonya, could you do something for me?" He looked down at her.

"I need to know what it is." She felt she ought to cry, she loved him so much.

"A sensible suggestion. I'll go back to my parents' home. You, I want safe in my apartment. It's a very secure building. This is *not*. Two girls in the lobby were only too pleased to let me through tonight. I could have been anyone."

"But you're not just anyone." She shrugged. "You're David Wainwright. I know the security on the building isn't tight. You Australians are so unsuspecting. I never let *anyone* through who appears to be waiting an opportunity."

"Very wise. And we Australians are not as unsuspecting as you think, though I concede we have been for a very long time. Do you want to pack a few things? I want you to bring the Madonna. I have a safe in the apartment. I think the icon should be transferred to a bank. Alternatively there's a strong room in my father's house. It could go there."

"It must stay with *me*," she maintained, her expression weighed down with a mix of powerful emotions.

"No one will take it from you, Sonya. But they very well could if you insist on keeping it here. Give it some thought now. If you truly believe Laszlo has never ceased searching for you, you've put yourself into the frame through association with Marcus. That makes us in our way responsible."

"You will go to your parents' house?" she questioned him, her green eyes searching his face.

"That's a promise. You have nothing to fear from me. I would never harm you."

"Maybe you harm me already," she confessed. "I'll go with you, David. Give me a few minutes to pack a bag."

He saw them the instant they came through the security door. His target and the tall, strikingly handsome young man who had been at the funeral and had walked her to her car. He knew who he was. David Wainwright. A member of a mega-rich, highly influential family. He looked superbly fit. He moved like a top athlete. Nevertheless he thought, if he had to, he could take him. He himself was as fit as any man could be, although he gave this Wainwright fellow a good ten and more years. Confrontation was clearly to be avoided. They were getting into a small nondescript car. Thousands of them on the road. He would follow them to their destination. They weren't going out for the evening. Wainwright was still wearing his dark suit but she was dressed in jeans and a white T-shirt. Even then she looked a countess.

CHAPTER NINE

DAVID had the entire top floor to himself. Sonya was coming to an understanding of what it meant to have a great deal of money. His harbourside apartment, a short distance from Lady Palmerston's, was sophisticated, clean lined, contemporary taste, stunning aboriginal art works glowing from the walls.

In the living room she saw several large sofas. The longest would comfortably seat six. It was positioned against the majestic backdrop of Sydney Harbour in its night-time dazzle. A half a dozen comfortable armchairs were covered in willow green; two bucket chairs upholstered in a complementary soft mustard suede.

The living room was divided from the dining room by a series of substantial wooden columns. The dining setting, with a rectangular mahogany table, meticulously crafted, was for ten. Adjacent another smaller setting for six, this time around a circular table. She could see he loved fine timbers as much as she did. The splendid mahogany flooring was bordered by a polished limestone inlay. It was all very impressive. A far cry from her apartment.

"You'll be safe here." David's eyes followed her slender, willowy figure as she wandered about.

"I love where you live, David. I love your style." She spoke calmly enough, but inside she was shaking. They were alone together inside his apartment. One part of her longed for him to sweep her up and make love to her. The other commanded her to hold herself together.

"That will do for a start," he said, his tone sardonic. "There are four bedrooms apart from the master suite. Come and see where you think you'll be most comfortable. All the guest rooms are made up, bed linens changed once a week whether I have guests or not. All of them have en suites. Sonya, come along." He knew he sounded in full possession of himself, but hunger for her was nearly bringing him to his knees.

"Where are we going to put the Madonna?" she asked.

"First things first, I see. I have a safe in my dressing room."

"May we put it away right now?" Her emerald eyes were fixed on him with great intensity.

"Of course. Follow me. I recommend you pick out your bedroom first. You get the icon out your bag. I'll go open the safe."

"You don't want me to know the combination?"

"If I give it to you, you have to guard it with your life," he returned.

The shorter the time they were inside the confines of his dressing room, off the bedroom, the better. One false move and she would be right into his arms. That couldn't happen. He had given his promise.

Sonya was so on edge she picked the first guest room they came to. He put out a hand to flick the panel that controlled the lighting. Immediately the room glowed with soft golden light. The room had an exceptional view of the harbour. There was a big king-sized bed, with a dark golden bedspread, a long, very interesting mahogany bench at its foot; a big comfortable armchair with a good-sized footstool. A long Japanese scroll framed in ebony over the bed; a plush coffee-coloured area rug imprinted with Japanese-style branches and blossoms in a soft chocolate.

"Your guests must count themselves very lucky," she said. "This will do me fine."

"Okay." He made himself walk away from her, fighting down urges that were mounting into a tremendous force.

"David?" she called, after a minute or two.

His name on her lips was a caress. "Are you lost? I'm down here at the end of the hallway."

He sounded so matter-of-fact she might have been a young cousin. These tumultuous emotions could well be on her side. She had to remember he would have had any amount of experience with women. She had had no sexual experience along the way. She moved slowly, almost pinning herself to the wall. She had to think of Marcus. There was no other way.

His bedroom was huge, again with the magnificent view and a spacious balcony beyond. The neutral colours were given considerable impact by a splendid dark crimson and gold bedspread. Matching cushions sat on the two big armchairs positioned on either side of a coffee table. On it stood a specimen vase, with a single pure white butterfly orchid with three delicate stems. A bronze bust of a beautiful woman was nearby.

"My mother," he said, following her gaze.

"She's very beautiful." Sonya moved closer to inspect it.

"That she is," he said. "I take after my mother's family, the Holts."

She stroked the sculpture with a gentle finger. "I can see *you* in the set of the eyes, the high cheekbones, even the mouth."

"I resemble my mother, yes. Come along, Sonya. We'll get this icon into safekeeping."

He spoke so crisply she had the dismal feeling she was holding him up and he wanted to be away from her. The dressing room was adjacent, beyond that the bathroom, all in keeping with the subdued opulence of the rest of the apartment.

She bent her head to kiss the case reverently, speaking a few words in Hungarian. It had been a source of family pride for her grandmother to teach her mother the language of her birth and for her mother in turn to pass that language on to her. Through her father she had learned to speak fluent French and German, just as her mother did. It had been nothing in her family to speak several languages. It had been encouraged. She passed the icon to David, watching him in silence as he put it into the safe, built into the floor of his mahogany wardrobe. The room had the smell of luxury, of leather and beautiful clothes.

"Thank you, David," she whispered.

"Let's get out of here."

There was a dark, intense look on his face. "You wanted to bring me here," she pointed out, turning about almost at a run. "Now you think you've made a mistake?"

"Maybe I have!" He moved after her.

"So the Madonna is safe! That's all that matters. I don't have to stay. I'm happy to go back home."

"Are you?" He swung her back to face him, as wound up as she. There was a fierce quaking locked up inside him that threatened to escape. A telltale shaking was travelling down his strong arms.

"I want to be as much away from you as you want to be away from me," she said fiercely. "Isn't that so?"

In her fury she looked incredibly beautiful, eyes blazing like precious gems, hot colour in her cheeks. "How many times do I have to tell you? I *want* you, Sonya. But I'm trying to do the right thing. Don't make it impossible for me. I hardly seem to know what I'm doing any more."

"And you hate it, don't you?" she accused "You want to fight it, this first time a woman has the better of you?"

"The better of me?" His handsome face tautened. "I'd advise you not to provoke me, Sonya." He felt panicked by his rush of anger. Only it wasn't anger at all. It was white-hot desire that was burning out of control.

Her eyes went huge in her emotion-charged face. She knew her behaviour was verging on the irrational, but she couldn't stop. "Why, would that give you an excuse to rape me?"

Shock and disgust froze his tall, elegant body. "I'm going to have to forget you said that, Sonya," he said, *too* quietly. "I'll go now. But before I do I'll show you how to lock up after me."

The words were barely out of her mouth before she realized how disgraceful they were. Some men wished to rape. David, never, never, never! She flew after him. "David, I'm sorry. So sorry. I didn't mean that. You are right to despise me."

"Good night, Sonya," he said curtly, without looking at her.

"Please, David, don't go in anger. I said I'm sorry." She had feared all evening she would cry. Now she did, seeking any measure of relief from the tightening knots of pain.

He swung back on her, looking incredibly tense, his eyes as black as night. "Don't *do* that. I don't want you to cry. Wait until I'm out of here."

"Yes, of course." Obediently she dashed the tears away with one hand, then perversely went back on the attack. Nothing made sense. "Who are you to give me orders?" she demanded. "I'm allowed to cry if I want to. Now, what is it you wish to show me?" She tilted her chin, wanting to prove her self-control hadn't gone with the wind.

Her dramatic volte-face got under his guard. Women! he thought in high frustration. "Come here." He motioned her towards a large panel of switches.

"I think I know how to handle a few switches," she told him with that infuriatingly blasé aristocratic air.

"You *don't* know." He gritted his teeth, feeling like a man lurching towards disaster. "Just listen and watch."

She didn't dare move a step closer. A step closer to this man she loved with all her heart. She had known little certainty in her life, but she knew *this*. "I fall in love with you," she burst out, flooded with all sorts of conflicting emotions. "It is all wrong, a catastrophe. I know you think that."

He felt like hitting something in his immense frustration. He knotted his fist, then hit the wall. "Sonya—"

"Every time I see you I fall deeper in love," she confessed, a writhing mass of nerves. The floodgates had well and truly opened. "A tragedy. I didn't want it. I don't even understand how it has happened."

"Sonya," he said very tightly indeed. "I *must* go."

"Go, then. Go, *go go*!" She was utterly beside herself, almost dancing on the spot. "I put up with you as long as I can!"

She was sounding more and more foreign, her excellent English failing her.

He couldn't afford to continue this argument. Didn't she know she was inciting him beyond control? "This one," he gritted, stabbing his finger to a switch. "Then this one." He pointed to a switch in the next line. The slightest spark would set him off.

"So you're going to abandon me?" she cried.

Was she a woman gone crazy sending out all these

mixed messages? He stared down into her overwrought face "Abandon you? Excuse me, you wanted me out!"

Do something, for God's sake. Do something for both of you. The voice inside his head shouted the warning.

"Don't go, David." Now she turned to pleading. "I hurt you. I am sorry."

"Sonya, if I stay—" He broke off, dragging breath into his lungs like a marathon runner.

"Stay," she whispered. "You want me. I want you. I want to lose my virginity to you. I promise you I won't regret it."

The drumming in his ears was so loud he had to put up his hands to cover them. The voice inside his head was no match for this heavy pounding. "Sonya," he groaned, under unbearable pressure.

"It's all right." She went to him, lifting her white slender arms to link them around his neck. "Kiss me, David."

It was a heartfelt plea. Yet her voice was more *alluring* than any woman's had the right to be.

"Hold me. Make love to me."

Such an invitation was like a galvanic electric charge. What man could deny himself promised rapture? He knew he was in thrall to her. Woman, the goddess. Man was right to fear her. Only he didn't hesitate to obey, not for a nanosecond. He swooped to lift her high in his arms.

For a moment as she opened her eyes Sonya was disorientated. She had no idea where she was. She was lying in a huge, wonderfully comfortable bed, stark naked. Then on a wave of heat it all came flooding back...

David!

She put a hand to a pink nipple. It throbbed. She found herself stroking her own skin with a sensuous hand. She had never felt more like a woman. She was a virgin no longer. She was in a state of euphoria.

David! She whispered his name. *David, her perfect lover!*

Rolling voluptuously onto her back, she stared up at the high plastered ceiling. The world felt like a different place. It was transformed. David had made love to her, starting so slowly, sweetly, gently, so exquisitely mindful of her, so when at long last, when she could stand no more, they joined together her deliriously excited body was ready for him.

"Forgive me," he had murmured, drawing back to stare at her, showing his distress.

Forgive? What was there to forgive? He had shown her unimaginable rapture. Afterwards both of them had sunk into a spent sleep, her naked body spooned into his, his strong arm around her. Both had awoken at dawn when they made love again, this time in an escalating desire that became a passionate fury. She had lost her heart totally. He had wrung the soul from her. Now her body was his. Every inch of it he had charted. She had thought sex something she could live without. She knew very differently now.

It was David who had now to take control of the situation. Could they become a couple? Could she ever be accepted? There were so many hurdles to be covered. But whatever happened in the future no one could take her night of nights from her. It had been a sublime experience. David had made it so. She wanted no other man.

He almost missed her coming out of the apartment building. She must have called a cab because she flagged it down as it approached the luxury complex. He had to be getting old. He had fallen asleep after he saw Wainwright drive away some hours before, in a big Mercedes.

She was on her own. That was good!

All he needed to do was follow her. He had a hunch she was returning to her own apartment. A hunch that was soon proved correct. No question the two of them were sleeping together. Why not? They were young, beautiful people. He didn't want to hurt this girl. He was Hungarian. He knew all about the tragedies of the Andrassy-Von Neumann family; the tragedies that followed after the war. He knew how the car crash that had killed the girl's parents had been engineered. He had never wanted such a job. He wasn't a murderer, but he did know the name of the man who had done the job. He had proof the count was a bad man. A scary man, even to him who had been given the job of scaring people. Only this young woman was the true countess, the rightful heir. Once all those things had mattered a great deal to him, but for years now he had been corrupted into becoming just another one of the count's pawns.

Sonya paid off the driver, then made for the entry to the building. She needed to pack more things if she was going to be away from her apartment for some time. David wanted her to stay at his apartment, but eventually they had decided it would be best for her to move in with Lady Palmerston, who had instantly agreed to having her.

Almost at the front door of the building she became aware of the footfall behind her. She turned, seeing a big, burly man, well dressed, advance towards her. His demeanour, however, was in no way threatening. He addressed her in Hungarian. Somehow she wasn't shocked. She had been expecting it.

"Good morning, Countess. At last I have found you."

His tone was respectful. Sonya replied in the same language. "What is it you want?" Her green eyes were cold and distant.

"Only to speak to you, Countess." He gave a half-bow. "Have no fear. I mean you no harm. There is no point in running away. I will always find you. Let us get this over. I come as an emissary from your cousin, Laszlo. He has a proposition to put to you. Allow me to put your mind at rest. He means you no harm."

She gave a bitter laugh. "Like he meant my mother and father no harm, I suppose?" At this time in the morning there was no one around. Most of the tenants, young people, would be at work. She was very much on her own.

"Please don't be frightened." He took a step back so as not to crowd her. "We will go up to your apartment. We will talk. I think you will be very happy to hear what the count wishes to offer you."

"There is *nothing* he could offer me," she said, with cold contempt.

"Please, Countess. Upstairs. You can't get away from him. I promise you I mean you no harm. Neither does the count. Violence is to be avoided at all costs."

"Only because he knows he wouldn't get away with it. I have spoken to important people about him."

"Upstairs, Countess," he insisted. "It is just a matter of delivering the count's proposal. Then I will leave."

Oddly she believed him. Perhaps some residual sense of decency, of honour remained.

It was just as she thought. Laszlo wanted the Madonna. In return he would pay into the bank of her choice, anywhere in the world, the equivalent of ten million dollars.

"It is a very good deal, Countess. You could be rich!"

Her expression was totally unimpressed. "Laszlo must be mad if he thinks *I've* got it."

The man shook his head. "But you have, Countess. Give

it up. You're a beautiful young woman, you have your whole life in front of you. Why should an icon mean so much?"

"You know very well," she reprimanded him, sternly. "You are Hungarian. Our religious icons mean a great deal to us. How do you know you won't be punished for trying to take it away?"

He laughed without humour. "I'll be punished if I *don't*!"

"Not if Laszlo is in jail."

He shook his head. "That won't happen, Countess. He has too much power. He will hunt you down wherever you go. Call him off. Let him have the icon."

"Perhaps I need the money first?" she said, with a cool lift of her arched brows.. "He *is* family, but a monster."

"So give him what he wants. Do you have it?"

"Certainly not *here*," she said. "I'm not a fool. Money first, then maybe we'll talk. He should be able to arrange an electronic transfer very easily. I can give you the name of my bank and the number of the account."

"A wise decision, Countess." The man stood up, a handsome man in his fashion, his blond hair almost sheared to the skull and penetrating blue eyes.

"How shall I contact you?" Sonya asked.

"Do not worry, Countess. I shall contact you. All that matters in life is to stay alive. It has been an honour to meet you. The Andrassy-Von Neumanns were once one of Hungary's greatest and most noble families."

When he arrived at the house, Angie, the housekeeper, told him his mother and father were enjoying a late breakfast.

"No need to announce me, Angie. I'll go through."

"I'll make fresh coffee," Angie said, hurrying away.

The informal dining room, well proportioned and expensively furnished, faced onto beautiful gardens of which his mother was enormously proud. "What is it, David?" his father looked up to ask. "You're on your way to work?' He studied his son's tall, lean figure. David was wearing one of his beautifully tailored business suits. He was well known for being a very smart dresser. "You needn't go in, you know. Nigel can hold the fort for a while."

"Have you had breakfast?" his mother asked, always happy to see her adored son.

"Angie's making me some coffee." He sat down, his briefcase on the floor beside him. "I have something to show you both. It needs to go into the safe room. It belongs to Sonya. I've also organized for her to stay with Rowena. She's not safe where she is."

His father regarded him with a puzzled frown. "Really, David, spare me the cops and robbers. What is it you've got? What could the girl have that needs to go into a strong-room?"

"You'll see in a minute." He reached into his briefcase. "What I'm going to show you has been in Sonya's family since the seventeenth century."

"Really? Sure she's not making it up as she goes along?" Sharron pursed her lips. Yet, Rowena, nobody's fool, trusted this girl.

"I think this will persuade you." He unwrapped the icon slowly, and then set it down gently on the table.

"And that's it?" His mother sat back, arching her fine brows. "An old case?" Only the binding had the patina of centuries.

He opened out one side, then the other. Sunlight was splashing through the tall windows into the breakfast room. He manoeuvred the case into a brilliant ray.

"Good God!" Robert Wainwright leaned forward, stunned. "A religious relic, obviously Roman Catholic."

"Where on earth did she get this?" His mother looked

every bit as stunned as her husband. "The diamonds are of the first water." She touched an exquisitely gentle finger to the array of diamonds in the Madonna's crown. "The precious stones are gorgeous too. The stones alone would be worth a great deal of money. How did a young woman who works as a florist come by this?" She searched her son's dark eyes.

"Go ahead, David. Tell us," Robert Wainwright said.

David did.

Afterwards his parents, their attitude greatly changed, made the decision to have Sonya's cousin investigated. "I'll make the necessary phone call right away," Robert Wainwright said. "There shouldn't be any difficulty tracking the Andrassy-Von Neumann family since 1945. Actually I know of the count. He's an industrialist and an extremely wealthy man."

David was back in his office when a phone call came through from Rowena. She sounded agitated, which wasn't like her. An involuntary spasm gripped the area around his heart. Surely Sonya was safely at home with Rowena? Even as he thought it he knew Sonya to be highly unpredictable. She had spent much of her life taking risks. He had been wrong to believe she would stay put.

"Sonya is here," Rowena told him at once. "She's had a rather frightening experience this morning."

He gripped the phone harder. "But she's okay? She hasn't been harmed in any way?"

"No, dear. I should have told you at once. But you must hear what she has to say. Is it possible for you to get away?"

He was already on his feet. "I'll be there shortly."

"Thank you, darling." Rowena made a sound of utter relief.

His first guess was Sonya's stalker was in town and had made contact with her. The Madonna was safe in his father's strongroom. His father had already started the investigative ball rolling. Not for the first time he was very grateful for the power and influence his father had.

His secretary came to the door, an anticipatory look on her face. She loved her job. "Have Prentiss bring the car around to the front of the building Liz," he said with some urgency.

"Onto it!" Liz moved off, never one to waste a moment.

They all sat in Rowena's garden room. A tense little group.

"Don't tell me, I can guess." David searched Sonya's face. "You've had a message from Laszlo via an intermediary."

She was enormously comforted by his presence, even if he was looking so formidable, such a tautness in his expression. "He treated me with respect," she said in an effort to allay his fears.

"Then he can count himself lucky," he clipped off. "My father has made a few phone calls. He knows of your cousin, Sonya. He's an important industrialist."

A lofty disdain came into her face. "Even important industrialists can be corrupt. Corruption is everywhere in high places. Massive fraud. Corporations with their meaner than mean streaks, robbing people, dismissing legitimate claims and getting away with it. It happens all the time."

"Well, you can leave the Wainwrights out of that," he said, leaning in closer to her.

"Hear! Hear!" Rowena piped up. "I've often wondered

what it would be like to be a victim I saw so many sad things in the old days. This Laszlo would seem to be a very bad boy indeed."

"He had my parents killed." Sonya started to rock herself, her arms crossed defensively across her body. "His man offered me ten million dollars for the Madonna. Blood money." Her voice broke.

"But S-Sonya!" Rowena was seriously taken aback.

Sonya met David's eyes. "No big thing! I already have twenty, don't I?"

He knew now to ignore the challenges she threw out. They were defence mechanisms. Her behaviour at different times was indicative of her perilous and erratic past life. "Indeed you have," he said in a calming voice. "So what is your thinking on this, Sonya? You get the money in, but you keep the Madonna."

"How did you guess?" She gave a little laugh. "Of course I keep the Madonna. It is *mine*! I give the money away to a just cause. Homeless young people, I think. You can help me there, David."

He sat studying her, an intent look on his face. "Do you like putting yourself deliberately in danger?" he questioned. "You don't seriously believe this Laszlo is going to let you get away with it?"

"He will just have to, won't he?" She gave the characteristic lift of her chin.

"My dear!" Rowena was starting to panic. She had come more and more to realize what a very difficult, even dangerous life Sonya had led.

Sonya could see neither of them was happy with her plan. "The man who visited me practically admitted Laszlo was responsible for the death of my parents." Tears stood in her eyes.

"How absolutely shocking!" Rowena was as astounded

by Sonya's story as David's parents had been, although she had known from the beginning Sonya was a young woman of breeding.

"I always knew it," Sonya told them painfully.

"But what is needed is hard evidence, proof, Sonya." Vertical lines appeared between David's black brows. "This man won't speak to the police. The last thing he needs is to have his cover broken. And what about Laszlo? He's a man who has long operated without ethical boundaries."

"So you're against me?"

He moved from his chair to where she was sitting on a two-seater sofa. He took her hand, keeping it within his own. "Listen, stay cool. You've had an upsetting experience. We're *all* on your side, Sonya. But I'm not about to tell you you've done the right thing pretending you were prepared to strike a bargain. How can you trust this man anyway? He's a hireling."

"He had nothing to do with the death of my parents, David," she cried. "He's Hungarian. I *knew* he did not intend to hurt me."

David was by no means certain of that. "But then he believed you, didn't he?" he countered. "He thought you had seen sense. How did he say he was going to contact you?"

"He didn't say. He's been watching me all along."

David's expression heightened to trigger alert. "So it's likely he knows you're here with Rowena?"

Her beautiful face showed her dismay. She looked across at Rowena. "I am so sorry, Lady Palmerston. The last thing I want is to put anyone in danger. I'll go home."

"Of course you won't!" David, deeply perturbed for her, spoke more crisply than he intended. It was obvious Sonya was in a highly emotional state. He couldn't have her rushing off on her own. It was out of the question. On the other hand, he felt he could no longer leave her with Rowena. Rowena wasn't a young woman. The safest possible place for Sonya was at his parent's.

Sonya didn't take kindly to that. He knew she wouldn't. "No, thank you, David," she said, with a positive shake of her head. "I can't think your mother is as sympathetic towards me as you say. Besides, I have nothing to fear. This man will not hurt me. The Madonna will protect me."

It seemed more than his life was worth to tell her not to count on it. "Okay, so I have the house watched 24/7." That should be easy enough, using their security people.

"You think that's necessary, David?" Rowena asked. "There's an excellent security system in place here."

Sonya turned her green eyes on Rowena. "You would feel a whole lot better if I were away from here, Lady Palmerston, wouldn't you?"

"Nonsense, dear," Rowena said firmly. "Our aim is to protect you."

"Let's slow down a minute." David held up an authoritative hand. "Dad has spoken to the commissioner. We should leave it to the police to come up with a plan. That's their job. That's what they're trained for."

"I don't need their help, David," Sonya said, starting to get nervous at the talk of police intervention.

"You *do*," he flatly contradicted, intensely concerned for her safety.

Her white skin flushed. "You're angry with me?"

He exhaled a long breath. "I'm *worried*, Sonya, as I should be. This man must have given you quite a fright coming up behind you, for all you're trying to hide it."

"Worse things have happened to me," she said. "It can be simple, David," she appealed to him. "I wait to get the money. I give it away. It's mine anyway and plenty more besides. I am the rightful heir. I will tell this man I will not lay claim to the Andrassy-Von Neumann estate. He can have *it*. Monster that he is, I know he will take care of it. He has a son. Probably grandchildren. Maybe they are not monsters?"

"We'll soon know if they are," David said wryly. "No one is ever going to hurt you while I'm around, Sonya. When the police come up with a plan I won't be very far from your side."

He stood up purposefully. He had many things to do. Sonya stood too. He put his arm around her. She closed her eyes, nestling against his shoulder.

"You're my world, David," she said, very softly.

He hugged her slender body to him, resting his chin on the top of her head.

They presented quite a tableau. Rowena, looking on, fell back against her armchair. Her face, so concerned, broke into a smile of pure delight.

My goodness me! So that's how the land lies!

She couldn't have been more pleased. Brave Sonya nursing a dangerous secret for far too long would come through all her pain and loss with Rowena's splendid nephew beside her. In his own way, dear Marcus had begun the healing process. Only destiny had its own plan for Sonya and David. It had reached out and touched them with a magic wand.

Could there be anything more satisfying than a happy ending? Rowena thought. But first there was business to attend to…

CHAPTER TEN

A SHAGGY-HAIRED young man, with a mobile glued to his ear, paid little attention to him as he walked through the security door as the young man was walking out, still talking into his phone. How foolish these young people were to assume he had legitimate business in the building. The fact that he dressed smartly must have confirmed he was an all-right guy.

He had no problem either with the lock on the countess's door. Routine, performed without even trying. Within seconds he was in. He knew where Wainwright had taken her. He knew he had time to make a thorough search of the apartment. From long experience he would leave no sign he had been there. He could have told the count the icon was not in the apartment, but the count listened to no one.

Twenty minutes later. No icon. He wasn't a man who was easily unnerved, but he was wary of the fact the countess now had powerful people on side. And this was *their* country. That gave them a big advantage. The Countess Sonya was like no one he had ever known. He admired her, her illustrious name. He came from an impoverished family. He had left an abusive home as soon as he could, living on the streets, surviving by using his wits and his physical strength. Ten years before Count Laszlo Andrassy-

Von Neumann had recruited him, hearing of his "talents". The count was a man with no conscience who thought nothing of monstrous deeds as long as he didn't have to carry them out himself. A couple more jobs would set him up. He would quietly disappear to where even the count wouldn't be able to find him. The count was a disgrace to his ancient name.

They were having a quiet dinner together; a small out-of-the-way restaurant, but the food and the service were good. The entrée had just been taken away when Sonya's mobile rang.

She stared across at David, her eyes gone wide. "It must be him."

"Answer it," he said, knowing there was a trace on her mobile.

She sucked in her breath. "Hello," she said with enviable calm. A second later, she indicated to David with her hand it was the call they had been expecting.

David listened to Sonya as she spoke, his eyes not leaving her face. She looked and sounded perfectly in control. That told him so much about the dangers she'd had to endure. He couldn't understand a word of it. She was speaking Hungarian, as the voice at the other end must be. Was the same nationality a bond? He had to hope so.

The count's emissary delivered his message in a quiet, respectful voice. "You will know now, Countess, your cousin has kept his part of the bargain." That was true. The money had arrived in her bank, very probably to their great shock with more shocks to come. "Now we arrange the transfer of the icon, Countess." He kept up the homage. "You have it?"

"Of course." Sonya's eyes remained fixed on David's

striking face the whole time she spoke. His presence steadied her, made her feel near invincible.

"I need to have it in hand tomorrow," the man said.

"Then I suggest we meet at the Archibald Fountain in Hyde Park."

"The time, Countess?"

"Make it lunchtime." The timing had been pre-arranged. "Say, one fifteen p.m. People about, enjoying their lunchtime break."

"You come alone."

It wasn't a question. "Of course." She spoke haughtily, as if insulted he would doubt her word.

"No back up people, Countess. No Mr Wainwright. I play fair with you. You play fair with me. We both know the count isn't the man to cross."

"We both know he's a murderer," Sonya returned, stung into speaking passionately. "Even if he paid some criminal to do it. *You*, do not be late. I very much dislike being kept waiting."

"That will not happen, Countess." He broke the connection.

Her hands were shaking as she put her mobile away.

"Sonya," he exclaimed, hating what was happening to her.

"It's all right. I know this because you are with me."

His dark eyes glittered. "It's where I intend to stay," he assured her. "I got the Archibald Fountain bit, the rest was, well—Hungarian." He gave her a half-smile.

"David, I don't want this man to be arrested." There was appeal in her sparkling green eyes.

He couldn't answer for a minute, he felt so angry. "Sonya, why not?"

She watched as his expression turned tense. "I don't

want to cause him trouble. I do not have a bad feeling about his man. He has been most respectful. I know he hates Laszlo."

"He *works* for him, Sonya." David packed a whole lot of warning into his words. "Don't get carried away here. You can be certain this man had done some pretty terrible things. You cannot trust someone like that."

She inhaled a shaky breath. "Perhaps. I don't know." She shook her head. "People get forced into living bad lives, David. You have had a life of peace and privilege."

"You think I don't know that?" He pinned her gaze. "But I don't believe I could have been corrupted into a life of crime."

She offered her hand across the table. "Sorry, sorry. I stupidly offend you. All I'm saying is I do not believe he wants to hurt *me*."

He caught her fingers, with a groan. "Sonya, he will do what he has to. That's why there's a plan in place. The immigration department would like to have a little chat with your Mr Metzger. We have the name now. Or one of his names."

"Like *me*," she said, with a strange little smile. "Sonya Erickson, Sonya Von Neumann. A few in between. Once I changed my appearance with brown contact lenses. I could hardly see through them."

He looked back at her very gravely. She was wearing a short dress of silvery lace, very feminine, very seductive. No jewellery except for a silver bracelet and crystal drop earrings, high heels on her feet. She looked incredibly beautiful, the light shimmering off her radiant skin and hair. "Let's go," he said abruptly, holding up his hand to signal for the bill. "I'm desperate to make love to you."

Her emerald eyes suddenly held a tantalizing female taunt. "So, your place?"

"Where else? The truth is I can't bear to have you out of my sight."

Once inside his apartment they succumbed to the driving need that was in them. The *thrill* of it!

"I could die for this," Sonya moaned. They were helping each other undress, throwing clothes about without thought or care. The frustrations of being apart, the inherent dangers of the situation Sonya had found herself in, provided an ever more passionate coming together. The tempo of their kissing, the frantic embraces mounting to a symphonic pitch. Nothing had ever felt so *right*!

She was stretched out on his bed, her long, slender legs falling gently outwards like the petals of a flower. "Do you love me?"

His answer came in an instant against her open mouth. "Really, you don't know it already?" In a strange way this level of ecstasy was a form of torture, but both of them were meeting their feelings head-on.

"Perhaps I need more convincing?" She was gasping with pleasure.

"I've never known a woman remotely like you. You like to torment me, don't you?"

"You mean like *now*?" She reached down to lightly stroke him with her hand. His skin was like velvet.

He drew in a deep shuddering breath in response. "Marry me, Sonya," he said through shivery, ever-mounting waves of pleasure. "One thing though, my love. I'll never allow you to do the disappearing act."

She rolled atop him. "So you think I would ever *want* to? Are you *crazy*?"

He held her hips, staring up into her highly charged face. "You want the truth? It's *yes*! I'm crazy about you. Marry me, Sonya Von Neumann. I want all the world to see how much I love you."

She lowered her upper body into his, feeling the wild thud of his heart knock into hers. "You honour me," she said, pressing her mouth to his cheek. Then she lifted her blonde head about to make her important announcement. "I will take on the job of being Mrs David Wainwright."

"For how long?" He laughed in triumph. "You won't escape me, Contessa."

"For ever," she proclaimed. "I *love* you."

"I love you too. If I lost everything I possess, I'd still be the richest man in the world."

"So, *I* look after you," she said.

Afterwards they sat in his huge bath together, his tanned feet hooked around her white hips. The peaks of her breasts showed dusky pink through the foaming, *chypre*-scented water. David had the softest white towelling wash cloth in hand. He turned her this way and that, marvelling at the softness and the white perfection of her skin. He worked the washer over her face, her throat, her shoulders, her breasts, tipping her head forward onto his shoulder so he could rub her back. Then he made her stand up very slowly in the white foaming water.

"Aphrodite rising out of the sea foam!" he crooned. "All you need is a scallop shell." Naked, her long hair pulled into a careless knot, she looked dazzlingly beautiful.

Afterwards, she lifted her arms as he wrapped her in one of his big bath towels, and then he carried her back to his bed. There was a marvellous range of ways to make love. They could try them all.

* * *

A perfect cloudless blue, the sky was reflected in the waters of the fountain. People strolled through the leafy park, admiring the splendid playing fountain, others sat on benches or spread themselves out on the plush green grass enjoying a packed lunch. A few like him were out jogging the paths. Police in everyday clothes were stationed in the area. He couldn't pick them and he had tried. He hoped Metzger couldn't either. He thought his own disguise wasn't all that bad. Navy vest, navy jogging shorts, a wide navy band with a green and white logo worn Indian-style around his forehead. At least it kept the sweat from running into his eyes. He had refused to be left out of this. Sonya was too precious to him. He had made that very clear.

He was slowing up beside a big blazing flower bed when he saw a tall, powerfully built man approaching Sonya. The man was wearing a trendy straw hat pulled down low on his head.

Metzger. An internal alarm went off.

Immediately he leaned down and yanked at a strap on his joggers. Nothing wrong with the strap of course. The police would have been following his movements around the park as well, probably having a laugh. All of them knew who he was. It had been agreed he could join in the action but only if something went very wrong. It was not anticipated anything would. Sonya and the target would be surrounded.

Metzger raised his straw hat to her. "Good afternoon, Countess. Well met. You have the icon?"

She shook her head. "Did you seriously imagine I would hand it over to my cousin?"

Metzger, for a career criminal, looked positively astounded. "But, Countess, you have the *money*. Why would you do this? It's madness."

"Why? Why should *you* ask me such a thing?" Her

green eyes flashed. "The icon is a family treasure. It has been in *my* family for hundreds of years. *I* am the rightful heir, not Laszlo."

It was obvious Metzger was poleaxed and he didn't try to hide it. "I understand what has happened to you, Countess, but you could be in great danger. *I* will most certainly be in danger."

Sonya was acutely aware of that. "What do you need to disappear, Mr Metzger?" she asked. Against all the odds, she felt compassion for this stranger. Probably he had led a terrible life, but she felt there was some good in him.

"A lot of money, Countess." Fear had crept into his voice. "Your cousin would consider I had committed treason. In his own way he is *mad*. He would have me followed for the rest of my life. I must *go*!" He thrust out a hand to her and that was when several things happened at once.

David put on such a burst of speed he was onto Metzger within seconds, taking him down headlong onto the grass. The country's greatest footballer couldn't have executed a better tackle. Brawny as he was, Metzger found himself groaning in pain. To have been overpowered so easily was devastating to a man like him. Someone very strong had a hard foot rammed into the middle of his back. His mouth was filled with grass clippings, making him splutter.

Four plain-clothes policemen tore across the park, converging on the scene with ear-splitting shouts of, "Police!"

They took over from David while a crowd of bystanders stared in astonishment at the drama in progress. It was first thought to be a scene from a cop show, but there were no television cameras in sight. This was real life. But nothing sensational was happening apart from that spectacular tackle. Gradually they dispersed with the sensation of a let-down, going back to finish off their lunch.

The irony was, Metzger had only been planning on saying farewell to the countess he had found he couldn't harm. It was fast established he was unarmed. Regardless he was taken away, if not cuffed. He was informed he was not being arrested. He was simply being taken in for questioning. The investigation into Count Laszlo Andrassy-Von Neumann and his activities was already under way. Metzger, along with his numerous aliases, was Andrassy's known henchman.

Left alone David gathered Sonya in so tight an embrace, he might have decided not to let go of her at all. "Promise me, promise me you won't do this sort of thing again," he implored with a shudder.

She spoke in a soft, appeasing tone. "I knew he wouldn't hurt me, David. But *you* hurt him." A laugh escaped her.

"We did hit the ground rather hard," he said wryly. "How was I supposed to know he was just trying to say goodbye?" His arm around her waist, he began to walk her out of the park up towards High Street.

She gave him a teasing little smile, feeling such ease, such peace, such a new certainty in life she was luminous with it. "You look very sexy in your little jogging shorts," she commented. "Such an outfit displays your superb body."

"Well, *you* would know all about that." He hugged her to his side. "When we get our lives sorted—very soon, I hope—you can come jogging with me."

"Don't think you would have to give me a start. Well, not much of a one. I am very fit too."

"Top of the class!" He had witnessed how much courage she had. There had been no evidence Metzger would have wished a target safe.

They walked on, both feeling immense relief this part of proceedings was over. "What is going to happen to

Metzger, do you suppose?" Sonya asked at length. "I don't want Laszlo to be able to get to him."

He stared down at her. "*You*, wicked girl, are the one who refused to hand him over the icon," he scoffed. He was, in fact, rather in awe of her stand.

"I know, I take the money," she admitted, without regret. "But it's *my* money. Money Laszlo stole. We will give it away. Maybe I will give some to Metzger so he can go hide in some place Laszlo can't find him. Brazil, somewhere like that."

"Antarctica might be better," David said, very dryly. "You can't give the guy money, Sonya. He fell for you. Simple as that. Had you been plain with buck teeth he might have acted differently."

"No one has buck teeth in Australia," she said, taking him seriously. "All the orthodontists, the health care, the parents making sure their children grow up beautiful."

"Be that as it may, it's as I've told you before—beautiful women have a lot of power. You only have to consider what you've done to *me*."

"So I prepared a spell!" For so long she had thought true love would elude her. Only it had been waiting for her all along. "I intend to keep the recipe to hand for the rest of our lives," she told him, with her lovely smile.

David slowed their progress to a halt, feeling humbled by the strength of her commitment. They were standing beneath a magnificent shade tree. Dappled sunlight flowed over her in a stream; birds sang, love lapped them around. "*Eternity* would be better," he said in a voice that thrilled her.

"You don't care what some people might say about me?" She searched his dark eyes.

There was an incredulous lift to his brows. "Say *what* about you?" He held up her chin, bent his dark head to kiss her lovely upturned mouth. "All they can say is David Wainwright is madly in love with Sonya Von Neumann and they're going to be married early in the coming year. Does that suit?"

She could have cheered aloud. Never more to have to *hide*. "More than you can *ever* imagine! I love you, David. God has been very good to me."

He caught up her fingers, kissed them. "He's been very good to *me* too. I might even consider turning religious."

"*I* am," she told him quietly.

"I know, my darling!" Tenderly he drew her into his strong protective arms. "I think we might take in Hungary on our honeymoon. What do you think? Word is your cousin could be spending his future behind bars."

"Amen to that!" Sonya said fervently, laying her radiant head against his chest. The steady beat of his heart resounded in her ear. This was the heart that beat for *her*. "He deserves punishment. He is a destructive man."

"Well, it appears very much like he's going to get what's coming to him," David said with grim satisfaction.

"I do feel sorry for his family." Sonya, so happy herself, could find some forgiveness in her heart.

"Not your problem, darling." He kissed the top of her head. "You have *me*."

"That is the *greatest* thing!" she said, truly believing it was. "I have absolute faith in you."

Arm in arm they walked out of the golden green shade, into the bright sunlight. The dazzling prospect of an even brighter future awaited them, David thought. His heart was overflowing with love and a wonderful renewed sense of purpose. There is only one way to handle life, he thought. Take it firmly in hand. Focus all one's energies on accomplishing *good*. He loved Sonya as he'd never thought he would be lucky enough to love a woman. He had a huge job ahead of him as his father's heir. It wasn't all a life of privilege. It was hard work with the extra burden of responsibility. Many hundreds of lives were dependent on Wainwright Enterprises. The drive forward mightn't be easy at times, but his love for Sonya and hers for him made all the difference in the world. He felt himself a man truly blessed.

EPILOGUE

THREE months later Sonya was enjoying morning tea with Sharron, her mother-in-law, and Rowena when Robert Wainwright rang to give them some stunning news just to hand. Count Laszlo Andrassy-Von Neumann, who had been deeply embroiled in investigations into his affairs in the United States, Europe and Hungary, had been killed when his car had crashed into a tree on the Andrassy-Von Neumann estate in Hungary. Investigations were ongoing but suicide was a strong theory. The count had been known to have been deeply depressed and outraged by the multiple attacks against him; especially from people within his ranks who had come forward. The count was survived by his son, Miklos, and his four grandchildren, all of whom lived happily in the United States.

It wasn't until David and Sonya were almost a year into their idyllic marriage that the whole matter of the rightful heir to the Hungarian estate was at last resolved by the courts. Sonya's American cousins didn't want any part of it. They had all suffered from the ruinous stories that came out about their father and grandfather. Judgment was handed down. Sonya Von Neumann-Wainwright, the claimant, was the rightful heir.

It was Sonya and David who decided the palace and

the beautiful grounds of the estate would be opened to the public like many other stately homes. Permission was given for the palace to be used for grand functions. Laszlo had begun the reconstruction. It would take five more years for the palace and the grounds to be restored to their pre-war glory. In this way, tradesmen and craftsmen were to enjoy years of steady, well-paid work. Everyone from the government down took great pride in the restoration of one of Hungary's grandest national treasures.

During this time Sonya and David, his parents, and Lady Palmerston made frequent visits. They had become a closely knit family; even closer when Sonya conceived her and David's first child in the splendour of the master suite. Robert and Sharron now had their first grandchild. It was an occasion for great rejoicing. The child was named Stefan, after Sonya's father.

The man, Metzger, who hadn't been detained long by the police, mysteriously disappeared, never to be heard of again. Obviously someone had given him help and very likely an injection of money to get away.

Who?

Harlequin® *Romance*

Coming Next Month

Available May 10, 2011

REQUEST YOUR FREE BOOKS!
2 FREE NOVELS PLUS 2 FREE GIFTS!

◆ Harlequin®

Romance

From the Heart, For the Heart

YES! Please send me 2 FREE Harlequin® Romance novels and my 2 FREE gifts (gifts are worth about $10). After receiving them, if I don't wish to receive any more books, I can return the shipping statement marked "cancel". If I don't cancel, I will receive 6 brand-new novels every month and be billed just $3.84 per book in the U.S. or $4.24 per book in Canada. That's a savings of at least 15% off the cover price! It's quite a bargain! Shipping and handling is just 50¢ per book in the U.S. and 75¢ per book in Canada.* I understand that accepting the 2 free books and gifts places me under no obligation to buy anything. I can always return a shipment and cancel at any time. Even if I never buy another book, the two free books and gifts are mine to keep forever.

116/316 HDN FC6H

Name	(PLEASE PRINT)	
Address		Apt. #
City	State/Prov.	Zip/Postal Code

Signature (if under 18, a parent or guardian must sign)

Mail to the **Reader Service:**
IN U.S.A.: P.O. Box 1867, Buffalo, NY 14240-1867
IN CANADA: P.O. Box 609, Fort Erie, Ontario L2A 5X3

Not valid for current subscribers to Harlequin Romance books.

Are you a subscriber to Harlequin Romance books and want to receive the larger-print edition?
Call 1-800-873-8635 or visit www.ReaderService.com.

* Terms and prices subject to change without notice. Prices do not include applicable taxes. Sales tax applicable in N.Y. Canadian residents will be charged applicable taxes. Offer not valid in Quebec. This offer is limited to one order per household. All orders subject to credit approval. Credit or debit balances in a customer's account(s) may be offset by any other outstanding balance owed by or to the customer. Please allow 4 to 6 weeks for delivery. Offer available while quantities last.

Your Privacy—The Reader Service is committed to protecting your privacy. Our Privacy Policy is available online at www.ReaderService.com or upon request from the Reader Service.

We make a portion of our mailing list available to reputable third parties that offer products we believe may interest you. If you prefer that we not exchange your name with third parties, or if you wish to clarify or modify your communication preferences, please visit us at www.ReaderService.com/consumerschoice or write to us at Reader Service Preference Service, P.O. Box 9062, Buffalo, NY 14269. Include your complete name and address.

HRI1

*With an evil force hell-bent on destruction,
two enemies must unite to find a truth that turns
all-too-personal when passions collide.*

*Enjoy a sneak peek in Jenna Kernan's next installment
in her original* TRACKER *series, GHOST STALKER,
available in May, only from Harlequin Nocturne.*

"**W**ho are you?" he snarled.

Jessie lifted her chin. "Your better."

His smile was cold. "Such arrogance could only come from a Niyanoka."

She nodded. "Why are you here?"

"I don't know." He glanced about her room. "I asked the birds to take me to a healer."

"And they have done so. Is that *all* you asked?"

"No. To lead them away from my friends." His eyes fluttered and she saw them roll over white.

Jessie straightened, preparing to flee, but he roused himself and mastered the momentary weakness. His eyes snapped open, locking on her.

Her heart hammered as she inched back.

"Lead who away?" she whispered, suddenly afraid of the answer.

"The ghosts. Nagi sent them to attack me so I would bring them to her."

The wolf must be deranged because Nagi did not send ghosts to attack living creatures. He captured the evil ones after their death if they refused to walk the Way of Souls, forcing them to face judgment.

"Her? The healer you seek is also female?"

"Michaela. She's Niyanoka, like you. The last Seer of Souls and Nagi wants her dead."

Jessie fell back to her seat on the carpet as the possibility of this ricocheted in her brain. Could it be true?

"Why should I believe you?" But she knew why. His black aura, the part that said he had been touched by death. Only a ghost could do that. But it made no sense.

Why would Nagi hunt one of her people and why would a Skinwalker want to protect her? She had been trained from birth to hate the Skinwalkers, to consider them a threat.

His intent blue eyes pinned her. Jessie felt her mouth go dry as she considered the impossible. Could the trickster be speaking the truth? Great Mystery, what evil was this?

She stared in astonishment. There was only one way to find her answers. But she had never even met a Skinwalker before and so did not even know if they dreamed.

But if he dreamed, she would have her chance to learn the truth.

Look for GHOST STALKER by Jenna Kernan,
available May only from Harlequin Nocturne,
wherever books and ebooks are sold.

HNEXP0511

Fan favorite author
TINA LEONARD
is back with
an exciting new miniseries.

Six bachelor brothers are given a challenge—
get married, start a big family and whoever does
so first will inherit the famed Rancho Diablo.
Too bad none of these cowboys is marriage material!

Callahan Cowboys:
Catch one if you can!